Victory!

FORGET-ME-NOT

→→ *Barbara Haworth-Attard* ←←

FORGET-ME-NOT

Harper*Trophy*Canada™
An imprint of HarperCollins*PublishersLtd*

Forget-Me-Not
© 2005 by Barbara Haworth-Attard.
All rights reserved.

Published by Harper*Trophy*Canada™, an
imprint of HarperCollins Publishers Ltd

First edition

Harper*Trophy*Canada™ is a trademark of
HarperCollins Publishers.

HarperCollins books may be purchased for
educational, business, or sales promotional
use through our Special Markets Department.

HarperCollins Publishers Ltd
2 Bloor Street East, 20th Floor
Toronto, Ontario, Canada
M4W 1A8

www.harpercollins.ca

Library and Archives Canada Cataloguing in
Publication

Haworth-Attard, Barbara, 1953–
Forget-me-not / Barbara Haworth-Attard. –
1st ed.

ISBN-13: 978-0-00-639549-2
ISBN-10: 0-00-639549-X

I. Title.

PS8565.A865F67 2005   jC813'.54
C2005-902060-1

HC 9 8 7 6 5 4 3 2 1

Printed and bound in the United States
Set in Monotype Plantin

FOR ALL THE ORDINARY WOMEN AND MEN
WHO CALL UPON THEMSELVES
TO PERFORM THE EXTRAORDINARY.

Lawrence Haworth

The London armories, which for over five years have resounded to the tramp of fighting men's feet, last night were filled with the silent prayers of hundreds for the men who will not return . . .

—London Free Press, *Tuesday, May 8, 1945*

*One of these days [I] shall be boarding a ship for Canada.
One can never tell, that could be any time for we don't
know what is going to happen one day from another these
days. The Germans are crumbling on all fronts, running
out of ammunition and soon their back will be broken.*
—Lawrence Haworth, 1st Canadian Signals,
June 30, 1944

Monday, May 7, 1945

Late evening

THE WAR IS OVER! It's been five years, eight months, and six
days since Germany invaded Poland and war was declared.
We've lived with the war for so long, it doesn't seem real that it
is over. But it is. Here is what happened:

We were sitting in boring old History (old—isn't that a good
way to describe History?) when suddenly the door flew open,
banged against the wall with a crash, and Billy Simpson ran
into the room. Mr. Crawford whirled around from the black-
board and opened his mouth to yell, but Billy beat him to it
and shouted, "The war is over! Germany has surrendered!"

We all started screaming and jumping up and down right
there in the classroom. We were about to dash out without
even asking permission, when Mr. Crawford shouted, "Class!
Return to your seats! Recite Mr. Winston Churchill's speech."

We all groaned and plopped back down in our chairs.
Mr. Crawford is a great admirer of the British prime minister
and made us memorize one of Mr. Churchill's speeches that
we had to recite whenever Mr. Crawford felt our morale was
sagging. We half-heartedly started: "We shall not flag or fail.

We shall go on to the end. We shall fight in France, we shall fight on the seas and oceans . . ." And all of a sudden a thrill of pride ran through me and it must have run through the others, too, because we began shouting, "We shall defend our island, whatever the cost may be, we shall fight on the beaches, we shall fight on the landing grounds, we shall fight in the fields and in the streets, we shall fight in the hills." We ended by screaming, "We shall never surrender!"

Then we ran out of the classroom, not even bothering to pack up our books.

"This is real history in the making," Mr. Crawford shouted after us.

All down the school hall, doors flew open, and students streamed out, yelling and cheering. My ears were ringing from the noise! I found Nancy Goddard, and we ran right away to my house to tell Mother. Brian beat us home, but that didn't matter as Mother knew all about the war being over from the radio.

I told Nancy to call her mother from our house, but we couldn't get a telephone line out. Everyone in London—heck, everyone in Ontario and Canada—must have been telephoning one another with the news! Stephen came running in from the elementary school with David, John, and Harry Goddard right behind him.

"There's to be a big celebration downtown," he said. "We're taking our bicycles."

"Hold on there," Mother said. "No one is going anywhere until . . ."

But Caroline came rushing in with Baby Billy in her arms, and Stephen and Nancy's brothers tore out the open door.

"Stephen!" Mother called.

I knew he heard her, but he pretended he didn't. I wonder if Mother realizes the *influence* the Goddard boys are having on him! But then we all used to worry that Stephen was too quiet and timid, so I guess this *influence* is not so bad. (I am still collecting words for Alex—if only he was interested in them, but I've not lost hope.)

Anyway, then Aunt Lily came rushing in, still in her factory overalls, Grandma trailing along behind her. Our place was like Grand Central Station for a while with neighbours coming and going, everyone hugging and crying.

I don't know if it was Nancy Goddard's influence or not, but I thought this was a good time to make ourselves scarce. "We're off to the celebration," I said not too loudly, but loudly enough so that I could say I had told her if Mother protested later.

"Just one minute, young lady," Mother said.

I should have known. Mother hears everything!

"You should all be going to the church and thanking God for this victory," Grandma put in.

I nearly died on the spot. "Church!!!" I wailed. The biggest party in the world was taking place downtown and Grandma wanted us to go to church! Even Nancy didn't want to go to church, and her father is the minister!

"You can go to the celebration," Mother said.

I couldn't believe my luck. Usually Mother is so unfair, but I guess the excitement had her brain addled.

"That's swell," I said, pushing Nancy toward the door.

"But . . ." Mother said.

With Mother there is always a but.

"Brian will go with you."

I assured her we didn't need Brian and pointed out that Stephen went on his own and he's only ten, whereas Nancy and I are fifteen!

"Stephen is with the Goddard boys. They'll watch out for each other. Besides, it's different for young girls. Downtown will be crowded. People might get rowdy. There are all kinds of servicemen down there. Brian escorts you or you don't go at all," Mother said.

Honestly, just because we're girls we get stuck with him.

3

That hardly seems fair. I swear I saw Brian's chest puff up twice its normal size at that word, "escorts."

"I'll take good care of them, Mother," he said, all serious sounding.

Mother told Nancy she'd stop by the church and tell her parents that Brian was ESCORTING us. My plan was to ditch him first chance we got.

I have to stop writing, because my hand is falling off my wrist. I waved my flag too hard this afternoon. I wonder where Alex is? He is probably over the moon that the war is done. I expect he is with dumb Julia.

When Alex came home from the veterans' hospital last September, Mrs. Harding from church sent her daughter, Julia, to visit as part of the church's program to welcome returning veterans—though it SHOULD be called Mrs. Harding's program to marry Julia off.

Julia visited a few times, and even though Alex didn't say much to her, she kept coming. Julia is a very mousy girl: mouse-brown hair, mouse-brown clothes, squeaky mouse voice, everything about her is mousy. Her father owns a construction company and she works for him three days a week keeping his accounts. She and Alex began to go for walks together and to movies. I told Mother that there was no need for Julia to come any more, as Alex was much better and I could go for walks with him, but Mother said that Julia was good for Alex, and before I knew it she'd become his girlfriend. All I can say is that she is not at all what I would choose for Alex. He needs someone with more colour and *ambition*. I don't know what Alex sees in Julia! Now my hand is really hurting.

I guess everyone is happy back there in Canada. I see some of the big cities are making big Victory Day preparations for

when peace is declared. WE are all expecting to be home very soon after this ends and there will be some very happy fellows after spending 5 years away from home.
—*Lawrence Haworth, September 1944*

The greatest unplanned celebration in local history swept through downtown London yesterday in wake of news of victory in Europe.
—London Free Press, *August 8, 1945*

Tuesday, May 8, 1945
Morning

My picture is in the newspaper! Right on the front page!!! I'm in a junk wagon with a bunch of other kids from school on Dundas Street downtown, waving a flag madly. There's me and Nancy and stupid Brian behind us. Beneath the picture it says, "A group of high school students." Mind you, I'd rather be in the picture that is next to it of girls sitting on a jeep full of soldiers. Beneath that picture it says, "A guard of honour of beautiful girls." But the junk wagon picture is better than none at all.

"That poor horse having to pull all of you," was all Mother said when she saw the picture.

There were thousands of people downtown, cheering and waving flags. All the offices and stores (except those that sold flags!) were closed. People wandered all over the streets, so the police stopped cars from travelling through downtown.

Dad just read this from the newspaper to Mother: "Paper that ordinarily blushes unseen in the private interiors of city homes burst forth in streaming glory from the windows of downtown buildings." (I read over Dad's shoulder to copy that. It was too long to remember.) Now he's saying, "Stephen, go see if our paper is blushing in the private interior of the can.

Why can't they just call it what it is? Toilet paper! Blasted newspaper." Dad's touchy this morning, because he indulged too much last night.

We got back from downtown just before dark, because it started to pour rain, to find Dad and Mr. Turner from next door and Aunt Lily's boyfriend, Sam, with their arms wrapped around each other, singing "Rule Britannia." I was mortally embarrassed that the minister's daughter should see them like that, but Nancy just giggled. Worse is that I have a suspicion that Mother and Aunt Lily indulged also, because their eyes were quite bright and they giggled just like Nancy. Come to think of it, Mother is a bit touchy this morning too.

More about yesterday! It was the most amazing day of my entire life—so far. When we got downtown there were scads of people. And so noisy. Car horns blared, and noisemakers from New Year's parties screeched, paper floated in the air—even paper that blushes. A soldier grabbed Nancy, and gave her a big kiss—right on the lips! And he didn't even know her! After that Brian stuck to us like glue. I told him to get lost, but he just stayed! I waited and waited for someone to kiss me, but no one did! It's all Brian's fault. He *glowered* at anyone who came near us. I'm sure it was very off-putting.

Of course, I'm not sure what I would have done if someone had wanted to kiss me. I'd probably have had to push him away, and say quite kindly, but firmly, "I'm sorry, I can't kiss you. I'm promised to someone else." That is, of course, if I really am promised to George. It's so hard to know because he's back in Saskatchewan and I'm here. I mean, I'd rather he was in Saskatchewan than here sick in the hospital, but now I only have his letters to read—not him to talk to. At first I had trouble deciphering his letters as he was still learning to write with his left hand, having lost his right arm in the war, but his writing is much improved the last few months. He lied about his age and signed up when he was seventeen. He's nineteen now and studying to be an accountant because he says he can't be a one-armed farmer. The government is paying for his schooling through a special program set up for veterans. I'll have to look into that for Alex.

Last year, before George left London, he told me he'd be back on my sixteenth birthday to take me on a real date. Let me be crystal clear about this. HE really said that. I didn't just imagine it, like that time I thought Rick Anderson had asked me on a date—and he hadn't. I still blush when I think of that—especially when the ENTIRE school found out my humiliation.

I turned fifteen this past April 18, so I have almost a year to go until I see George again. But does that mean I'm promised to him? If so, I probably shouldn't let a soldier kiss me. Unless, of course, it is my patriotic duty to kiss a soldier or sailor or airman at Victory celebrations. I have no idea of the correct etiquette for this occasion. Maybe Dorothy Dix's advice column in the newspaper will tell me tomorrow. She knows everything about everything, even kissing. Drat it! I must have said that out loud, because Brian just said, "What are you mumbling about kisses?" I swear there is no privacy in this house. I'm going to my bedroom!

May 8, 1945

My bedroom

I forgot to say that Rick Anderson was the one who pulled me up onto the junk wagon. He really is quite good-looking.

Even more about yesterday! We met Betty and Lydia downtown and we all went upstairs at her father's bank and threw pieces of shredded paper from the windows. Her father gave us flags. Brian, Nancy, and I only stayed for a bit as it was much more exciting on the street. Betty made eyes at Brian the ENTIRE time. It was quite disgusting.

I forgot to say that today is Brian's seventeenth birthday. I remember last year when Brian lied about his age and enlisted in the army. Dad stopped him going, but I think that entire episode aged Mother about ten years. Mother just called to say I have to get ready for church to go to prayer services. I told her I didn't feel like going, but she said we were ALL (except Alex—he doesn't go to church any more and Mother doesn't make him) going, to remember Aunt Lily's husband, Uncle Billy, and the other soldiers who died in the war for our freedom and that I needed to remember that some people were not celebrating because a son or daughter would never come home from the war. She's right. I feel a most dreadful person right now. I vow in the future to not think of myself so much. Maybe Mother will let me sit with Nancy at church.

May 8, 1945

Evening

I am very tired from all the excitement. Half the time I feel like crying, and the rest of the time laughing. At church today Reverend Goddard read a psalm, "And now shall mine head be lifted up above mine enemies round about me." But then he said that we had to be careful not to exact revenge and start yet another bloodbath.

I'm surprised he doesn't want revenge when his son, Brent, has been a prisoner of war. I want someone to pay for the way Alex is now. He is so different since he came home from the war with battle fatigue. Even though he stayed at the hospital for months, and the doctors say he's better, he's not like my Alex from before the war. Alex used to be pretty much my best friend in this family. He stuck up for me when Brian teased me. He joked around a lot and made us all laugh. It's like a light inside him has gone out.

I can still remember the first time I saw Alex at the hospital after he was sent home from the war. He had a leg wound that we could all see, and another wound in his mind we couldn't see: combat exhaustion. It was caused, the doctors say, from seeing Uncle Billy killed right in front of him. For the longest time, Alex just sat there and wouldn't talk to any of us. He's better now and home, but is still very jumpy. Mother is always shushing Brian, Stephen, and me when we argue too loudly, saying it's bad for Alex's nerves. At least he's not diving under tables any more. When Alex first came home and he'd hear a loud noise, he'd dive under tables for cover. The first time he did it, we all crawled under the table too, scared something awful was happening, like a bombing.

I asked Alex this morning if he was excited the war was over. "I'm glad the dying has stopped," he said. "But it's not over. They might not be fighting any more, but it's not over for a lot of the men who fought over there, not for a long time, if ever. They will never forget."

Instead of going to the celebrations yesterday, he sat at Julia's house listening to the radio with her parents, which must have been very boring as Mr. and Mrs. Harding are pretty boring. So is Julia. In fact, their last name shouldn't be Harding, but Boring!

Last year I gave Alex the beautiful new diary Mother and Dad gave me for Christmas. Alex told me once he would like to be a *journalist* and I thought the diary might inspire him to get better and write. Instead he got a job at the aircraft factory with Dad and Aunt Lily. Even today he went to work at the factory so other workers could have the day off. Dad didn't go in. He said the factory only had a skeleton staff today to keep an eye on things. Ever since Dad said that, I keep picturing Hallowe'en bones working in the factory.

Now most people are saying to remember that the war is only half over—we still have to defeat Japan. I suppose they are right, but you could also say the war is half won, which sounds much better than half over. I do feel sorry for poor

President Roosevelt of the United States. He died April 12 of this year and never did get to see the end of the war. President Truman took over.

> *I still think Hitler is too much of a coward at heart to even shoot himself. All he strikes me as being is a man with the gift of gab. All his boasts and diabolical and tyrannous ways will come home to him when the Allies enter his gates of Berlin.*
> —*Lawrence Haworth, October 1944*

Wednesday, May 9, 1945

Hitler used to be a house painter! How on earth he ever became a leader of a country, I'll never know. The Nazis say he is dead, though the Allies have not found his body yet. He married Eva Braun just before the war ended. I can't imagine marrying such a monster. Dad says he thinks Hitler is still alive, but hiding like the coward he is.

Back to boring school today. After supper, Stephen and I went to Aunt Lily's and raked the garden so we can plant it in a couple of weeks. I wonder if I still need to plant a Victory Garden now that the war is half won? I guess so. I don't mind as I quite like my garden. I guess I really shouldn't call it *my* garden as it's Aunt Lily's backyard, but I'm the one who plants it and takes care of it because she doesn't have time, so I feel that makes it mine. I do share the vegetables I grow with Aunt Lily and Caroline and Baby Billy.

Thursday, May 10, 1945

There's to be a Victory in Europe dance at St. George's Hall tomorrow night. It costs twenty-five cents. Mother says I can go as it is a special occasion, and because Caroline is going, so she can keep an eye on me. Caroline is mooning all around, saying she met her Australian air force husband, James, at a dance at St. George's Hall. Though she and James didn't know each other very long, they certainly knew each other well enough to make Baby Billy! That is really a naughty last sentence.

What a relief it is that I finally know how babies are born. It's like being included in a special knowing club. I remember last year when I found out. I thought it was totally disgusting and vowed never to do that with anyone. I think now that it might be fine if you love someone.

At supper last night, Caroline kept saying, "I can't believe James will be coming home soon. I should start looking for our own place to live, because James won't want to live with Aunt Lily."

I noticed Mother and Dad exchange glances when she said that. I wonder why?

I curled my hair with Kleenex tissue tonight, because it is supposed to be patriotic to not use metal curlers. All the metal is to go to the war effort. I remember last year when Stephen stole all of Mother's cookware for the metal drive. It nearly drove her to distraction trying to find her pots and pans. I will say that the tissue is softer to lie on than metal curlers. I hope it works as I want to look good for the dance tomorrow night.

Friday, May 11, 1945

Late

Nancy is staying over tonight as the dance ran quite late. She thinks my bedroom is swell and I have to agree that it is quite *unique*. She says it is especially swell because her younger sister isn't in it. Nancy has nine children in her family! There are four girls and five boys, though one boy is just a baby, and Nancy's oldest brother, Brent, is in a POW camp in Germany. I know what Nancy means about sharing a bedroom. I used to share a room with Caroline and we fought a lot!

After Alex came home from the hospital last September, Mother and Dad thought it best that he have his own room, rather than share with Brian and Stephen. Caroline and Baby Billy live with Aunt Lily, so Mother and Dad decided Alex should have my room. The only place they could think to move me was the back sun porch. Dad tells everyone he fixed it up for me, but other than moving my bed and dresser down there, I don't see what else he did. Mother made scads of curtains to cover all the windows. I really didn't mind giving up my bedroom. I am just so glad to have my Alex home. Besides, I like having windows all around me, especially in summer when I lie at night and a sweet-scented breeze comes in and the crickets chirp. Mind you, it was pretty cold last winter, even though Mother left the door open to the kitchen to get some heat. On really cold nights, Dad moved my mattress into the dining room and I slept there.

The dance was fun. Betty and Lydia and some of the knitting club girls were there. Brian ended up coming with us, too! We girls had a great time dancing with each other, though at first I stood around looking mournful and tragic in the hopes that someone would ask why, so I could tell them about being promised to George who is far away in Saskatchewan (which I think sounds very romantic). But no one asked, so I decided to have fun.

Caroline only danced with Brian and Nancy and me. She said it was inappropriate for a married woman to dance with other men. (Since when did Caroline get so appropriate? I remember when she used to wear bright-red lipstick and go out every night!) Aunt Lily and Sam were there, too. I wonder if Aunt Lily will marry Sam. He's not as dashing as Uncle Billy (Uncle Billy looked like Clark Gable!) or as funny (Uncle Billy was always telling jokes). Sam's pretty ordinary looking with light-brown hair and mud-coloured eyes, but he's quite nice. Aunt Lily met him at the aircraft factory, where he works in the office. He has a hole in his heart that kept him out of the war. But I think Aunt Lily should snatch him up, heart problem or not, because there are quite a few widows and single gals around. I overheard some of the girls at the punch table complaining that the British women have snared a lot of our soldiers over there and married them. There's going to be a lot of spinsters in Canada!

Tonight reminded me of George, and my graduation dance that I invited him to. It wasn't a date, even though I invited him. Mother says I can't date until I'm sixteen. I should be getting his weekly letter soon. I wish Nancy wasn't sleeping. I'm wide awake, and it would be nice to talk about the dance, and George, and I also want to ask her about why she danced with Brian! She must have felt she had to because he's my brother.

By the way, Kleenex tissues do NOT make good curlers. I looked a fright this morning when I took them out.

Saturday, May 12, 1945

It is National Hospital Day today, when anyone can go and tour a hospital. Why they would want to, I certainly don't know! Hospitals are horrible, smelly places. Nancy and I were volunteer hostesses for the morning at the veterans' hospital, but only three people came to see around our floor and sunroom. Very dull. I could have told the hospital no one would come, but then no one asked me! Nancy had to go home right afterward to help her mother, so I went to the theatre with Betty and Lydia in the afternoon. We went to Loews and saw *National Velvet* with Elizabeth Taylor. She is very beautiful. I wish I was beautiful like her. Even if I was very beautiful, I'd still be nice to people—extra nice, so no one could say, "She's beautiful, but not very nice." People always talk about beautiful people like that.

They had riots in Cape Breton and Halifax on VE Day. The newspaper called them "Peace" riots. What's peaceful about a riot? I'm glad we didn't have them here during our VE celebrations. Mother and I are going to a Victory Concert at Beal School tonight, put on by a Russian choir. I wouldn't mind seeing a real Russian.

Saturday, May 12, 1945

Late

How disappointing. The choir wasn't really Russian. They were Canadians who are descended from Russians. I told Mother it was very misleading calling them a Russian choir when they come from Windsor, Ontario!

Sunday, May 13, 1945

Today is Mother's Day. I pinned a red tulip on my sweater to wear to church to show that my mother is still alive. I offered to make cinnamon toast and pancakes for supper as my gift to her, but Mother assured me she didn't mind cooking. Dad gave Caroline a small bunch of flowers. James had sent Dad some money to buy them. Caroline cried. I wrote a letter to George this afternoon and told him all about the VE celebrations and the dance and the movie and the dumb Russians who weren't really Russians.

If I had dimples I bet I'd be as beautiful as Elizabeth Taylor. I wonder if George would like me with dimples. I'll put a PS on my letter and ask him before I mail it tomorrow.

Monday, May 14, 1945

Cold, rainy day. Last year I had planted my garden by now, but this year it has been too cold. Dad says it's too bad because he really enjoyed planting his garden before Grandma last year and showing her his lettuce before hers had even sprouted!

We had knitting club after school. Nancy and I run it under the direction of our Domestic Sciences teacher, Miss Wormould. Honestly! That's her REAL name! Not one we made up. She should marry the first man who asks her just to get a better last name!

Betty has joined the knitting club now because her father said she had to. She's an even worse knitter than I was when I started! We have twenty-three knitters now.

Got a letter from George today. He says his studies in Saskatoon are going very well. He says no one back home on the farm can believe he is a college man. I never thought of this before, but I can tell the knitting club girls that I'm promised to a COLLEGE man. Betty and Lydia will be green with envy.

Tuesday, May 15, 1945

Still raining. My legs were red with cold by the time I got home from school. Nancy came with me. Brian hung around us until I told him to scram. Tried making dimples with the pointy end of a pencil while I sat in classes today. It didn't work. I just got sore cheeks.

> *Well, confusion today is for the Germans and for us hope and some thoughts for a better future.*
> —*Lawrence Haworth, December 1944*

Wednesday, May 16, 1945

Nancy's family got a cable saying their son, Brent, was freed from the German prisoner of war camp and has gone to England. Nancy is over the moon!

Thursday, May 17, 1945

Betty has a dimple-maker! She is going to lend it to me. Nancy says you can't make dimples, you have to be born with them, but I'm going to try it anyway.

Saturday, May 19, 1945

I got offered a job! A real grown-up job! One that pays money! When I went to the hospital to volunteer this afternoon, they asked me if I'd help wheel patients to treatments and the sun-rooms on Monday after school until 8 p.m. and every other Saturday afternoon. They said I was very mature for my age. I quickly telephoned home and asked Mother and she said I could if I didn't let my school work slip.

I know exactly what I'm going to buy with my first pay! There is the most adorable sundress pattern to order through the newspaper.

Sunday, May 20, 1945

I asked Mother if I could order the sundress pattern now and pay her back when I get paid. She said, "Don't go counting your chickens before they hatch." Honestly! She has a *trite* saying for everything. But then she said to go ahead and order the pattern.

Mother is a little bit cranky because she and Dad are having an argument. They're not arguing in front of us, but we can all tell they're fighting because Mother's lips get tight when Dad comes in the room and Dad makes a lot of noise shaking out his newspaper and hiding behind it. I wonder what they are fighting about. It can't be me because they don't mind yelling at me when they're mad.

I told George all about their silent fight in my letter to him this afternoon. Now that I think of it, Mother might not be pleased I told George about our family business. She's always saying, "What will the neighbours think?" Once when she said that, Dad started to get up out of his chair and said, "Why don't I just go ask them?" Mother pushed him back into his chair. Sometimes they act so childish.

Monday, May 21, 1945

My first day of work! I only had one problem. I was wheeling a patient to X-ray, and a very attractive young doctor accompanied us. I was so busy admiring the doctor's crinkly blond hair and gorgeous blue eyes that I ran into the door frame with the wheelchair! I was mortified. The doctor asked the soldier if he was hurt. The soldier said no, and the doctor said, "This time let's try to go through the opening, not the wall."

A group of student nurses arrived today to work as part of their training. I admire them so much in their crisp uniforms and quiet-soled shoes. They aren't much older than me. They live together in rooms in the nurses' residence, which must be a great deal of fun. It would certainly be better than living with my family! It is time I started thinking seriously about my future. After all, it's not as if I'm a child any more. I do have a job.

Tuesday, May 22, 1945

I've decided to become a nurse. I will be following in the hallowed footsteps of Florence Nightingale (that almost sounds like a church hymn), devoting my life to the sick and the suffering. I was practising walking sedately (nurses have to be very quiet so they don't startle the patients) while I put the vegetable bowls on the supper table this evening, and Brian said, "Why are you gliding around like an idiot?"

I started to snap back at him, but thought that Florence Nightingale probably didn't yell at her brothers (though I doubt she had any as annoying as Brian), so I laid a gentle hand on his shoulder and smiled at him patiently.

"What's wrong with her, Mother? Now she's grinning like a fool."

Even Alex laughed, which really hurt my feelings. I expect Brian to be nasty, but not Alex. Nurses have to endure so much.

Wednesday, May 23, 1945

Nancy Goddard's brother, Brent, has his picture in the newspaper. He's now on his way home to Canada. Stephen and I planted Aunt Lily's garden today after school. Dad planted his this evening after work as he said he didn't want mine growing before his. We both beat Grandma, who is planting her garden on Saturday.

Thursday, May 24, 1945

I was talking to Mrs. Turner next door and I noticed she had some pretty, tiny blue flowers in her garden. She says they are called forget-me-nots and complained that they grow like weeds every spring. I thought that the most exquisite name. Flowers have such romantic names—love-lies-bleeding, lily-of-the-valley, forget-me-not . . .

She said I was welcome to take some for my garden, so I dug out a couple clumps. Each flower has five delicate, deep-blue petals. I wonder why I've not noticed them before. Probably because I never noticed plants at all until I had my first garden at Aunt Lily's. I planted the forget-me-nots along the borders of the vegetable garden beside the alyssum and lobelia. Caroline and Baby Billy watched. Baby Billy is so cute now that he is walking, except he walked right across my garden and pulled up all the stakes that told me what each row of vegetables is! I told Caroline she'd have to keep him out of it, as now I don't know what are beans and what are peas. She got quite huffy with me even though I pointed out to her that my garden will give her and Billy fresh vegetables.

I was surprised Stephen wanted to help me with the garden this year. I thought he'd want to play with the Goddard boys. I think even if we weren't at war with Japan, I'd still plant a garden. There is something immensely satisfying about dirt.

Friday, May 25, 1945

I am reading Mother's *A to Z Home Medical Book* in preparation to be a nurse. I had no idea there were so many bits and pieces inside my body and that so many things could go wrong with them! Alex was complaining of an earache when he got home from the factory, and I told him it might be an abscess. He said he thought it was just an ordinary earache.

I got a letter from George today. He said I look quite fine without dimples. I, personally, still think I'd look better with dimples. I mean, you often hear people say, "Oh, look at the pretty dimples on that one." But you don't hear them say, "Oh that one looks fine without dimples."

Saturday, May 26, 1945

My second day at work. I'm so proud as I got everyone to the proper place today, with no mishaps. I had to stay late to take a first aid course in case of an emergency.

Five Women of Lidice [Czech Republic]
Only Ones Found Alive

. . . [T]here were 174 men rounded up. . . . [A] Gestapo man named Wiesman told the firing squad that it was the Fuehrer's will that the village should be destroyed. By 4:00 p.m. all the men had been killed, the women and children carried away in covered trucks and all the houses burned to the ground.

—London Free Press, *June 11, 1945*

Sunday, May 27, 1945

When will Mother understand that I am an adult? She treats me like I'm a child. Here is what happened:

After church in the morning, Nancy and I went to do our volunteer work at the hospital as usual. Even though Alex and George are no longer patients there, and I have my job on Mondays and every other Saturday, I still go to help out. As we were serving the ginger ale in the sunroom, the men began talking about the "atrocities" that were being uncovered in German-occupied countries. I asked Nancy what they were talking about. She seemed quite surprised and said hadn't I heard the rumours of death camps for Jewish and Polish people in Germany. I told her I remembered hearing something, but couldn't recall exactly what. She became quite exasperated with me.

"Did you read any further in the paper on VE Day than your own picture?" she asked.

I had to admit that I'd been so dazzled by my own *debut* in the newspaper, I hadn't. She said to read the next few pages of that paper and I'd see for myself. I tried to get her to tell me, but she said I should read it for myself. When I got home I asked Mother for the newspaper. I knew Dad had kept it as a souvenir.

"It's around somewhere," she said. She was busy peeling a potato. "Why?"

I asked her if she'd heard rumours of death camps in Germany. She pursed her lips and kept peeling the potato, but didn't answer right away. "I don't think it's suitable for young girls to be talking about such unpleasantness," she said finally.

"Well, Nancy knows all about it. And so do the people at the hospital! I have a job, Mother. They said I was quite mature. I'm not a child any more."

Mother held up what little was left of the potato. "Oh, now look what you made me do! Honestly, Bobby. Why are you always so much trouble?"

Sunday, May 27, 1945

Evening

I found the newspaper, but now I wish I hadn't! Maybe Mother is right—I'm not old enough to know this stuff after all. I feel sick. I can't even write about it right now.

> *The world will never know the exact total of human lives sacrificed to Germany's incredible program of mass extermination.*
>
> —London Free Press, *June 1, 1945*

Monday, May 28, 1945

I couldn't sleep last night, and I kept gulping back tears at school, so I left at noon and went to Aunt Lily's. I was scared to go home because Mother would know I'd played hooky. Aunt Lily was on night shift at the factory, so she was just getting up when I got there. I told her about the newspaper reports of how when the Allied soldiers arrived in Poland and Germany they found the Nazi murder camps. I told her about the horrible atrocities the German soldiers had inflicted on the Jews and

Polish prisoners at Buchenwald, how they'd burned them in ovens and gassed them. Millions of them. Millions! Even children! I could feel my hair lift on my scalp as I told them about it. Caroline sat holding Baby Billy tightly the entire time.

Aunt Lily said that was what our men were fighting against over in Europe. "That was why my Billy died, so that we could stop the Nazis and not become part of that horror," she said. "Every time I think it unfair that Billy died, I tell myself his death was needed to help stop these awful things happening overseas and to stop it from ever coming here."

I went and worked in the garden a little bit after that, pulling weeds from the rows until I had to go to my job. I don't understand how people could hate so much they'd want to kill other people. But at the same time I worry about how I feel. I don't even know a single German, yet I think I hate THEM for what they did to Alex, leaving his mind broken. It's so confusing. I must be an awful person to hate someone I don't even know.

Even though it's Monday and I just wrote a letter to George yesterday, I had to write him again tonight and tell him about the murder camps.

Tuesday, May 29, 1945

This morning Mother gave me a note to excuse me from school yesterday without my even asking. I guess Aunt Lily told her how upset I was.

But Mother did scold me and said that I am not to tell Stephen that the pain in his stomach is probably his appendix and he'll need an operation. She said she doesn't need me putting any more silly ideas in his head than are already there.

My sundress pattern came! Now I need money for the material to make it. Between buying Victory Bonds, and seeds for my garden, and going to the movies, I'm always short of money.

Wednesday, May 30, 1945

Before bed

Betty lent me her dimple-maker. She smuggled it to me in English class. I am wearing it right now. It is a headband made of metal that comes down to fit over the cheeks, held there by a chinstrap. Each end of the band has a little pointed cone that sticks into your cheeks. That's what makes the dimples. You have to leave it on overnight for a week to get results. I wore it down to supper to get a head start on my dimples, and everyone laughed. Even Julia, the brown mouse. I really don't think it is very polite to laugh at someone when you are a guest in their house! Brian nearly fell off his chair he laughed so hard and Dad wiped tears from his eyes. Grandma was over for dinner and said I was vain and I should accept the good Lord's handiwork as it was. I pointed out to her that she and other ladies wear lipstick to make the good Lord's handiwork look better. She told Mother I was a smart-aleck and would come to no good. Alex said, "We should have put you up against the Germans, Bobby. You would have confused them into surrender years ago." I really do have the most horrible family!

Thursday, May 31, 1945

Still no dimples. Prime Minister Mackenzie King is at the London Arena tonight to campaign for re-election. Mother and Dad are there right now seeing him.

★

German Prisoners Doing Farm Work

They left their camps at Glencoe at 7:00 a.m., 20 of them going to Port Talbot, where they will work at cutting logs in a bush.

—London Free Press, *June 14, 1945*

Friday, June 1, 1945

Exams are in two weeks. I saw an advertisement in the newspaper that says students can apply to be exempt from exams if they help farmers plant their crops. Too bad they don't exempt students who have jobs at the hospital. That's important work, too. Guess I'm going to have to study.

It said high school students can spend their summer vacation in a healthy environment and get paid! There is still a shortage of men to work for farmers, though I read in the newspaper that some of the German prisoners of war are being used in this area as farm labourers. I had no idea there were prisoners nearby. What if they escape? I must warn Mother to keep the doors locked.

I showed the advertisement to Brian, pointing out to him that not only would he miss exams, but he'd get great pay and be healthy into the bargain—and I'd get a peaceful summer without him around, except I didn't tell him that last bit. Brian said he had other plans for the summer.

Dad's shoulder is sore. I told him I thought it was *bursitis*.

Saturday, June 2, 1945

I tried to have a talk with Alex this morning. I told him that now that the war is half won, maybe it's time he left the factory job. I told him it was okay to work there while he was getting better, but he should be doing something more important, like writing for a newspaper like he said he wanted to before the war. He said the factory suits him just fine right now. He gets on well with everyone and the job isn't too demanding. I told him he should go back to school on the veterans' plan like George is doing. Alex became a bit testy at that. He said he appreciated my concern, but it really wasn't any of my business. He was quite shirty with me. I wanted to remind him who helped him get better by reading her diary to him, and visited him in the hospital, and gave him her NEW diary for his own while she wrote in an old math book, but I didn't think that would be very nice of me.

I also wanted to talk to him about a new girlfriend, one who has a bit of ambition for him. I'm tired of Julia squeaking around our house! But as he was so testy about the job idea, I decided to leave the new girlfriend until another day. I wonder if Caroline knows any nice-looking girls with a bit of ambition.

Sunday, June 3, 1945

Church this morning. Reverend Goddard in his sermon said, "Character is what you are in the dark." I guess that means I have to be good even at night when no one can see me! You'd think there would be some leeway to be a bit bad when a person is on her own.

Rick Anderson came over to talk to Nancy and me after church. He looked quite handsome in his Sunday suit. Then Brian came over to talk to us and suddenly I found myself walking home alone with Rick. Brian stayed to talk to Nancy. This afternoon at the hospital, I asked her what Brian and she were talking about. (I was worried they might be talking about me.) Nancy turned quite pink and said, "Oh, this and that. School, exams, you know."

Speaking of exams, I better get studying! I've left it quite long enough, but it's hard to do school work when the sun is shining and the air is warm.

Grandma and Aunt Lily, Caroline and Billy came over for

Sunday dinner. They walked, because Aunt Lily is having her car's tires retread as they are in poor shape. The war in Europe might be over, but you still can't buy new tires for cars because the rubber ration is still in effect—gas rationing, too.

But the bombshell was Aunt Lily's news that she and Sam aren't going out together any more. Before I could ask her why, Stephen burped! A huge burp! Right at the table. I can remember when Stephen was scared of everything, and how he'd crawl into bed with me, scared the war would come here. Now he burps at the table! Brian laughed, and Stephen put his hand in his armpit and made more rude noises. Dad and Alex started snickering, but Mother was just plain furious. "You do not make rude noises at the Sunday dinner table, Stephen," she said.

"Is it all right to make rude noises at *Monday's* dinner table?" Brian asked.

Everyone at the table laughed, except Mother. Steam almost came out of her ears. "That does it! You are just egging him on, all of you. Brian and Stephen, get to bed right now without any dessert," she said.

Stephen scampered off, but Brian said he wasn't a kid any more and she couldn't make him go to bed at six o'clock.

Dad told Brian to go clean the garage as punishment. Dad's been waiting for one of us to get into trouble because he's been wanting someone to clean the garage for him for two weeks.

"And you're not to tell everyone Mother said I was to go to bed at six, blabbermouth," Brian shouted at me as he left the dining room.

Wait until Nancy hears this!

Monday, June 4, 1945

Got a letter from George. He said the news of the murder camps had shaken up everyone because there were a lot of rumours overseas about them, but it wasn't until people actually got into

Poland and Germany and saw them first-hand that they realized the rumours were true. And in fact, conditions were worse than they had heard. He said he knew it was upsetting to me, but I should concentrate on the thought that the Allies stopped further deaths and further people being enslaved in labour camps. George is so sensible. I really miss him. I miss his lopsided grin, his thoughtful way of talking, his homely, yet not homely face.

Thank goodness I had knitting club and work at the hospital after school today, because Mother has decided to spring clean! I hate spring cleaning!

Still no dimples.

Tuesday, June 5, 1945

Nancy and I are to make a luncheon casserole in Domestic Sciences tomorrow for our exam. We've decided to make a salmon-and-potato bake with white sauce and cheese. Miss Wormould says it has to be *edible* to pass.

Mother made me help her spring clean after school. She made me wash all the baseboards. I asked her if Mrs. Turner next door was coming over later for tea and baseboard inspection, and Mother said Grandma was right, I was becoming a smart-aleck and I could also wash the windows to knock it out of me. Honestly, who looks at baseboards anyway?

My forget-me-nots are flowering beautifully. I think they are my favourite flower. I love the name. In fact, I signed my last letter to George with "Forget-Me-Not, Roberta," and I put in a dried forget-me-not flower I pressed between two pages of the encyclopedia. I signed it *Roberta* instead of *Bobby,* because I wouldn't want someone to find his letters and think a boy is sending flowers to him. Also enclosing the flower felt more like something a Roberta would do, than a Bobby.

Still no dimples despite my unfailing use of the dimple-maker.

Wednesday, June 6, 1945

I had a brainstorm today (a good one) and picked some chives from my garden on my way to school, and I'm so glad I did. For our exam in Domestic Sciences class we layered potatoes and salmon in the casserole dish. Next we made a white sauce, but the flour went all lumpy when we mixed in the milk, and then it caught on the bottom of the pan and burned a bit! We fished out the biggest black lumps and poured the sauce over the salmon and potatoes and sprinkled cheese on top. We left it cooking for half an hour. It smelled quite good, but tasted burnt—from the white sauce catching on the bottom of the pot, I guess. That's when I sprinkled chives on top—lots of them—and we passed! Miss Wormould said it looked very appetizing, then tasted it. She then murmured something about looks being deceiving, but gave us a ten out of ten for presentation, a two out of ten for flavour, and a six out of ten for nutritional value—though, as she pointed out, if it doesn't taste good the nutritional value doesn't matter much as no one will eat it. Still, we passed! Thank goodness for chives.

They say they found Hitler's body today, though some people think it isn't him and he is still in hiding. He committed suicide in one of his underground fortresses. Dad says only a coward like Hitler would take the easy way out and desert his "gang of goose-stepping goons!"

Brian was coughing today. I told him it was probably cholera, which is often fatal.

Thursday, June 7, 1945

After school, I went over to visit Aunt Lily. I asked her why she and Sam broke up. She said it was partly because she felt disloyal to Billy by dating Sam. I said that Uncle Billy was dead, and she said, "I know that, Bobby, but now that the war's over, it somehow doesn't feel right. I have so many questions. I'd like to ask Alex about Billy's last days, but I'm afraid of upsetting him. It's a confusing time for me right now."

I always thought when I was older I would know everything. That was one of the main reasons I wanted to hurry up and be grown up. I didn't expect to still be confused like Aunt Lily is.

She also said she doesn't know if she wants to be anyone's wife again, now that she's been working and out in the world and keeping herself. It really is too bad, because Aunt Lily is so beautiful, she could have any man she wanted and then she wouldn't have to work.

That reminds me. Lydia said she saw a newspaper article that a woman was told her husband was dead, and a year later she remarried. Then, a year after that, the woman was told her husband was alive, but in a prisoner of war camp! She had to decide which husband to stay with and she decided to stay with the husband she'd married first, as she felt he was a priority.

Betty wasn't at school today.

Dad's birthday. I bought him some more lettuce seeds. The rabbits ate all his lettuce as it came up and it made him hopping mad—a little joke.

No dimples yet.

Friday, June 8, 1945

Today was the best day of my life—so far. Here is what happened:

We had an awards assembly at school, where the dumb kids sit and watch all the smart kids and the sports teams get a crest and a letter. It went on forever, and I was in the middle of a huge yawn when suddenly I heard my name! At first I thought I was being called out for yawning, but then I heard Nancy's name and she wasn't yawning. I sat there with my mouth hanging open until Nancy grabbed me and dragged me up to the stage. "Close your mouth," she whispered.

I did, and next thing I knew I had a crest and a letter in my hand, and the principal told everyone that Nancy and I had started a knitting club after school and made a valuable contribution to the war effort. Let me be crystal clear about this, that's exactly what the principal said, "a valuable contribution." Then everyone applauded, and Rick Anderson stood and whistled. I still can't believe it! Especially when I remember how awful my first knitted sock was! Dad is so proud he's making me a special picture frame to put the crest and letter in.

Betty came back to school. I asked her why she wasn't there yesterday and she said she was "indisposed." I didn't know what she meant until Nancy whispered to me, "She had her period."

Then Nancy said that the best invention in the world would be if someone would make a better sanitary napkin. Betty said that was disgusting, but I completely agree with Nancy. With our panties, and garters to hold up our stockings, and then a sanitary napkin and belt, it's amazing we girls can walk at all!

I gave up on the dimple-maker. I guess Nancy is right and you have to be born with them.

I just thought about this! Betty doesn't have any dimples, so obviously the dimple-maker didn't work for her either. I wonder why she didn't tell me that in the first place. It would have saved me a lot of humiliation and sore cheeks.

Saturday, June 9, 1945

A trainload of wounded soldiers came in early this morning in hospital coaches with red crosses painted on their sides. Those men needing further care were sent to the hospital. I wheeled around a lot of people today.

Dad made me go with him to see Conservative leader John Bracken at Beal School this evening. Mr. Bracken is running against Prime Minister Mackenzie King in the election. Mother said I should go because it took women a long time to get the vote and it would be a good experience for me to be involved in politics. I noticed she didn't think it would be a good experience for *her*, because she stayed home. I don't know what all the fuss is about politics. I was bored out of my brain there. The only interesting part was when Mr. Bracken banged his fist on the podium and an old lady next to me nearly jumped out of her skin with fright.

I asked Dad who he was going to vote for. He said, "You don't ask people who they're voting for, Bobby, but probably King. He's the lesser of two evils." I didn't know voting was such a secret thing.

I have a rash on my arm. I hope I'm not getting diphtheria. I better look it up in my medical book and see if it starts with a rash.

Just looked it up: *Diphtheria symptoms: severe sore throat* (I swallowed a few times but my throat feels fine), *low-grade fever* (I think I am a bit warm), *enlarged lymph nodes (swollen glands) located in the neck* (I looked in the mirror and the right side of my neck is larger than the left), *painful, red, and swollen skin lesions*. I just swallowed again and my throat is a bit sore after all. I better go tell Mother.

Later

Mother says the only illness I have is an overactive imagination, and the rash is from pulling weeds in my garden. I'm sure she's right, but I see from the medical book it could also be eczema. Mother also said I better get studying for my exams and stop reading the medical book.

Sunday, June 10, 1945

At the hospital this afternoon while Nancy and I were volunteering, there was quite a lot of excitement. A German prisoner of war was injured at a farm outside of London and brought in for treatment. There was an armed man from the Veterans Guard outside the door to his room. (The men who are too old to fight, but still want to be part of the war belong to the Veterans Guard.) All the volunteers were told the prisoner's room was strictly off limits. One of the volunteers said she saw the prisoner come in, and he had on a blue coverall with red stripes down the pant legs and sleeves and a red bull's eye on the back! She said he had very shifty eyes, and a dreadful scowl on his face. I want to see what a German looks like, but I'm scared, too. In my mind they have devil horns and a forked tail, or else they are huge like monsters.

It seems some of the patients' families found out the hospital had a German POW and made quite a hullabaloo about him being in the same hospital as our boys. The hospital said they treat everyone who is ill, regardless of their nationality. I think that is very good of them, but I don't know if I could nurse a German. I try hard not to hate all Germans, but more and more horrible stories are coming out from Europe.

I saw a picture in the newspaper of children's shoes piled high in one prison camp—no children left to wear them. The Nazis had killed them all. They also beat and starved people until they looked like living skeletons. One radio announcer, his name was Ed Murrow from the United States, was quite upset about the concentration camps he toured. He reported in a broadcast that the Germans knew the horrible things that were happening to the Jewish and Polish people, and continued to work their farms and were well fed right outside the camps where people starved to death, and yet they did nothing. He says the Germans are now trying to pretend that they didn't know what was going on in their own country. He said they should have been outraged that people of their own kind would do such horrible things to other human beings. I wrote all about that in my letter to George today. I also told him the dimple-maker didn't work, so next time he saw me I'd still be without dimples.

Today is Baby Billy's first birthday. Caroline had everyone over to Aunt Lily's for a birthday party supper. Dad was thrilled, because Baby Billy called him "Pa." We were annoyed because all evening Dad kept making Baby Billy say it again and again, until Mother said, "Leave that poor child alone, Henry. You'll wear him out."

Brian, Stephen, and I are going to try to teach Baby Billy to say, "Bad Pa."

More than 90 London and district soldiers, back from the European battlefronts, arrived at the C.N.R. station here today. Relatives and friends, visibly moved at the first sight of sons and husband in many cases for as many as five years, rushed forward to greet the men . . .
—London Free Press, *June 1945*

Monday, June 11, 1945

Nancy's prisoner of war brother, Brent, is home! Here is how it happened:

Nancy telephoned first thing this morning before school (Dad grumbled who was ringing at such an ungodly hour, and Mother told him not to take the Lord's name in vain) to tell me that they had a telegram that Brent was on the train and would arrive in London at noon! Today! The military is sending the wounded and prisoner of war men home first. She wanted me to go with her and her family to the train station. She said she was terrified to see Brent, and I told her I knew exactly what she meant. When Alex came home from the war, I was terrified to see him at first in case he had an arm or leg missing and no one had told me!

Mother gave permission for me to miss school and go with Nancy to the train station. I love Mother! Then Brian said he would like to go too, though I have no idea why, and Mother said he could come with us. Then Stephen said he should go, but Mother made him go to school. She said Brian and I weren't to intrude on the Goddards' reunion with their son, but stand quietly by and help with the younger children if needed.

She also said that as it wasn't until noon the train was coming in, I could help her hang the drapes outside to air. I told her I thought that Nancy needed me at her house, and she assured me Nancy's family would be fine preparing for Brent's return without me. Brian looked as smug as the cat that ate the cream, but Mother dashed his smugness when she told him to get the ladder and take down the curtains for her. I hate airing curtains. The dust gets in my throat and hair!

We all crushed together in the automobile and went down to the train station. Mrs. Reverend Goddard had sent the three Goddard boys to school like usual, saying they are too excitable to keep track of in a crowd. That will make Stephen happy to know he wasn't the only one left out.

The train station platform was packed. There were ambulances and nurses to take the wounded to hospital, Red Cross women with tea, and some women from the new Eaton's War Service Depot that helps returning soldiers back to civvy life. There was also a band, a regiment of soldiers standing at attention, police to hold everyone back, and scads of other people to greet returning soldiers.

Then the train pulled in, and everyone started cheering. Even though I didn't know Brent, I yelled like mad. I thought I'd suffocate in the crush when the doors opened! The police couldn't hold the crowd back as we pushed forward on to the platform.

Suddenly Nancy shouted, "There he is." Then she started

sobbing. She clung to Brian and cried, "I never thought I'd see him again. I can't believe he's here."

I told Brian to put Nancy's head between her knees because she might faint. I read to do that for fainting in the *A to Z Home Medical Book*. Brian said I was nuts, Nancy was fine and not the fainting sort.

Then this tall, thin, tired-looking man came out of the train, and Mrs. Rev. Goddard dumped the baby in my arms and waved wildly. The man saw her and smiled and slowly made his way through the crowd toward us, so I guessed that was Brent. Mrs. Rev. Goddard, Nancy, and her three younger sisters clung to Brent, holding his legs and arms, whatever they could reach, nearly pushing him over, while Brian and Rev. Goddard held him upright.

It just occurred to me that Nancy grabbed Brian, not me, when she first saw Brent. Maybe Brian was just closer than I was at the time and Nancy was so *distraught* she didn't realize what she was doing.

Tuesday, June 12, 1945

Yesterday was election day. Mother and Dad voted. Prime Minister Mackenzie King won again.

Studied all evening for my first exam—History!

Wednesday, June 13, 1945

I overheard Mother and Dad having their silent fight, except this time it wasn't so silent. Mother said to Dad that they should really tell *her*, because "she needs to be prepared." Dad said no, let her enjoy the next while and that they would "cross that bridge when we come to it." Mother didn't seem very happy with that and argued with Dad a bit. I wonder who *her* is? I wonder if it's me? What do I need to be prepared for?

Maybe I'm really ill and dying? But it couldn't be diphtheria because I never did get a bad sore throat. I feel all right. I wonder what I'm dying from? Mind you, if I am dying, you'd think everyone would be nicer to me!

Thursday, June 14, 1945

Wrote my boring old History exam. Mr. Crawford says we're living history right now, so if that's the case, I don't think I need to know about Champlain or any of those dead explorers from a thousand years ago. I'll just live this history right now. Besides, if I'm dying what does it matter if I get a good grade or not?

Today is King George's birthday. I don't know how old he is, but he's old. About the same age as Dad, I think.

Friday, June 15, 1945

It's hot, hot, hot today. I thought I was going to melt on my way to school. We had a cold picnic supper out in the backyard, with fresh lettuce from my garden. Caroline and Baby Billy were over, and Grandma and Aunt Lily came too. And, of course, mousy Julia. I really must ask Caroline if she has any girlfriends for Alex. Julia had on a brown blouse today that made her seem more mousy than ever. She even nibbles her food. I once read a story about a mouse that had been turned into a person, but still exhibited mouse traits. Maybe that's what happened to Julia. I should mention this to Alex as he might not want a girlfriend who was once a rodent.

Dad said it was so hot out you could fry an egg on the sidewalk. Grandma said why on earth would anyone want to fry an egg on a sidewalk? Dad said of course no one would, but if they wanted to, they could. Just when I thought the conversation couldn't get any more boring, Dad and Aunt Lily and Alex talked about gaskets and screws and nuts and other dull factory stuff. I thought I'd die of *ennui* (a new word I discovered).

Mother made us drink every bit of milk she had in the icebox as there is little ice to be had anywhere because of the heat wave and she thought the milk would spoil. Now I know what a cow feels like before it is milked!

Wrote English Literature today, though I am sure it must be against the law to make students write exams in this heat. Caroline is waiting anxiously for a letter from James. She said she can't wait until he comes home. Mother glared at Dad when she heard Caroline say that, and I realized that Caroline is the cause of their silent argument, not me. Now that I think of it, how could they know I was dying when I haven't even been to a doctor in close to a year. But I wonder why Mother and Dad are fighting over Caroline?

I better warn Mother to be nicer to Dad. I read in Dorothy Dix's newspaper column that men do not like coming home after working all day to a poor atmosphere with bickering and quarrels. A man will often look outside the marriage for an agreeable, younger woman to make him feel like a boy again, and all a wife can do is keep herself well groomed, and be pleasant, until he comes to his senses and returns to her. Unfortunately, coming to his senses can sometimes take up to five years!

Grandma was complaining at supper that her foot hurt. I told her perhaps she had gonorrhea. Dad spluttered his potato salad all over the table and Brian fell onto the grass he laughed so hard. Mother said, "I'm going to take that medical book away from you, Bobby!" I have no idea what is the matter with them.

Late night

I looked in my medical book and I see what the problem is now! I meant Grandma had gout! No wonder Dad spit his potatoes everywhere—which, by the way, ruined dinner for everyone because no one wanted to eat their meal with Dad's half-chewed potato salad in it! Though I noticed Mother blamed me for the ruined meal, and not Dad! My only defence is that both the diseases start with G and were close together in the medical book, which lists ailments alphabetically. Anyone could have got them mixed up.

I folded the newspaper so Dorothy Dix's column about husbands was face-up right beside the Mary Hastings Housewife column that mother always reads. I'm sure the household hints, recipes, and penpals in the Mary Hastings column are all very fine, but I think it more important that Mother keep Dad happy.

> *The memories of eggs, fresh vegetables, such as lettuce, tomatoes, celery, etc. still are in my memories from back in Canada.*
>
> —*Lawrence Haworth, August 1944*

Saturday, June 16, 1945

Brian, Stephen, and I were invited to lunch at the Goddards' today. After Stephen and Nancy's brothers went outside to play, Brent told us about being a prisoner of war. It was terrible. Mrs. Rev. Goddard cried a lot while he spoke. Here is what happened to Brent:

Brent's plane was shot down over France. He and his crew parachuted down safely, but were immediately surrounded by Germans. They and a bunch of other prisoners were crammed inside a rail car that used to carry cattle. The prisoners managed to pry one of the doors of the cattle car open to escape by jumping, but the train was moving too fast. Then the Germans saw the open door and nailed it shut. They stayed in that car for four days before they arrived in Germany. Brent said the car stank to high heaven by the time they arrived at the

POW camp (they didn't have any toilets!) and he was completely flea-bitten from dirty straw on the floor of the car. He said the most horrible sight greeted them when they got off the train in Germany.

"The Russian and Polish prisoners, both men and women, hadn't an ounce of meat on their bones and their clothes were in rags. They could barely stagger to unload rail cars they were so weak, yet still that German guard's whip came down over their shoulders."

At this point Mrs. Rev. Goddard thought that Nancy and I should leave, but Nancy assured her we were fine, and I nodded, though I really wasn't sure if I was fine or not. My stomach felt a bit funny and I was having trouble taking a deep breath.

Anyway, Brent said in the prison camp their hands were tied or handcuffed all the time because the Germans said the British and Canadians were tying German POWs' hands, so they did the same. But one of the prisoners discovered that the key off a meat can could open the cuffs, so they'd take the cuffs off whenever they wanted, and then quickly put them back on when the guards came around.

He was fed bread and water and every third day a cup of cabbage soup. He said at night he would look out the one window in their barracks to see the stars and he kept thinking about how they would also be shining over his family in Canada. That thought, he said, was what kept him sane. I told him that's exactly what I had said once, that I wondered if the stars I saw were the same ones that watched over Alex and Brent, and that Rev. Goddard had said the stars were God's eyes watching over all the soldiers fighting.

"So that's why I found them so comforting," Brent said. "Thank you for watching the stars, Bobby."

I was really embarrassed, but I also felt good, like I'd helped him, even though I knew I really didn't.

Mother is calling me to set the table for supper. I'll finish this later as there is lots more to tell.

Saturday, June 16, 1945

Evening

Betty called to see if I wanted to go with her and Lydia to the pictures tonight, but I told her I was busy. I want to write the rest of Brent's story before I forget. Here is what happened next:

Brent said he worked making bricks in a factory, and most of the prisoners worked slowly or made lousy bricks to slow the German war effort down. He also chopped down trees and worked on the railroad. He said that the Russian women prisoners had to lay railroad tracks down by hand. The women were so hungry that if any soup from the English prisoners was spilled on the ground, they'd lick the dirt to get some, as they weren't given any food. It was the brutality toward the Russian and Polish prisoners and the senselessness of it all that Brent said made him the angriest.

The prisoners had radios they smuggled in and they heard about D-Day. Brent said after that some of the German guards began to be nice to them, as they were afraid the tables would be turned and they, the Germans, would become the prisoners.

Just as Brent finished saying that an odd thing happened. One of the Goddard boys came in to get a piece of bread and butter and he accidentally spilled a glass of milk. Brent got very upset and yelled at him that he was wasting food, and didn't he know people were starving? Rev. Goddard put a hand on Brent's arm, and he seemed to come to his senses then, and said he was sorry. Mrs. Rev. Goddard mopped up the mess. It sort of scared us all. Rev. Goddard said perhaps that was enough for today, but Brent insisted on continuing. "I need to tell you so you understand," he said.

I didn't want to listen any more, but I couldn't stop.

One day in the middle of January, Brent said guards came and told them the prisoners were being evacuated. He only had time to grab a blanket, some tea, and a frozen Christmas cake that Mrs. Rev. Goddard had sent him before they were forced to march away. He said the temperature was below zero, and snow was mounded high along the roadside. He said they kept passing men who had frozen to death at the side of the road.

After fifteen miles of walking, Brent stopped and leaned against a snowbank to catch his breath and a guard put a gun to his head and said, "Get up and march, you swine, or be shot." Brent said he got up pretty quick and went on.

I asked, "Where were they marching you to?"

"Nowhere," Brent said. "We marched six hundred and fifty miles to nowhere. They just kept us going around and around in circles, trying to escape the Allied armies that were getting nearer."

At this point, Brent began to pace up and down. Mrs. Rev. Goddard was quite distressed.

The first night was spent out in an open field. They were not allowed to have a fire and their boots were frozen to their feet.

(I have to stop to get a handkerchief as this next part makes me cry.)

"The socks you knitted me, Bobby, saved my feet," Brent said. "I had only two pairs with me, and one of them was yours. When we stopped for the night, I would quickly change my wet socks for dry ones and put my boots back on so my feet wouldn't freeze solid. I put the wet socks under my shirt to dry them while I walked."

If I ever see my old Domestic Sciences teacher, Mrs. Ford, again, I'll thank her for teaching me to knit!

"After several days we finally arrived at a POW camp at

Görlitz. Hanging at the gate was a wire cage, and inside was one of my crew. There was no room for him to stand or to sit with his legs stretched out. He was being punished for attempting to escape."

Brent's voice wobbled and he couldn't speak for several minutes. Nancy shoved a handkerchief in my hand. I hadn't even felt the tears on my cheeks. Rev. Goddard put his arm around Brent and held him close for a few minutes. Even Brian had tears in his eyes.

Brent said they left the prison camp and kept marching, and this time some inmates from a concentration camp marched with them. He said they had no shoes, but they walked barefoot through the snow.

And the whole time, Brent said, you'd hear gunshots as some men could go no farther, or tried to escape. Every fourth day they would get a bit of bread to eat. They marched for three months in the cold and snow to nowhere.

"So many died. But I kept thinking of you all at home waiting for me and I kept going."

One night they were put in a farmer's yard to sleep. "I woke up because someone was yelling that the Americans were here. The German guards were gone, so we all ran out and there it was! A jeep with three Americans in it. And here I am," he finished. "I lived, and here I am."

Sunday, June 17, 1945

I began to tell Alex about what happened to Brent, but Julia stopped me. "I don't think Alex wants to hear about this right now, Bobby," she said. And she was right. I hadn't noticed Alex begin to shake while I was talking. I felt so awful making Alex upset. I can't even be mad at Julia for stopping me because she was very nice about it. Later she came and told me to not feel bad (how did she know I was even feeling bad?)

because any kind of upset or hearing about terrible things starts Alex shaking. I guess Aunt Lily will have to wait a while longer before she can ask him about Uncle Billy dying.

Darn! Why did Julia have to be right? I wrote it all down for George in a letter instead because I had to tell someone or I'd burst. Even though Brent's story made me feel queasy at times, I was glad I heard it, as it helped me to understand a bit more why Alex is like he is. I wonder if all the soldiers are upset inside and it's just that some hide it better than others, or are some not bothered by war at all? I put a PS in my letter and asked George about that, too.

It was Father's Day today. Mother made him a chocolate cake (his favourite) and Grandma brought him ice cream. I've never seen Dad so happy to see Grandma. He loves ice cream.

Spent most of the day studying for my Geography exam. I didn't even volunteer at the hospital today because I had so much studying to do.

Sunday, June 17, 1945

Evening

Stephen fell off his bicycle after supper and scraped his knee and elbow badly. I pushed everyone out of the way and said I'd take care of him as I was a nurse.

Brian said, "You're not a nurse."

"I've been reading the *A to Z Home Medical Book* and I've taken a first aid course," I told him.

"That doesn't make you a nurse," Brian argued.

"I still know lots more than you about ailments," I yelled.

At which point Mother came out, picked up Stephen, and started toward the house. "While you two are fighting," she said, "Stephen is bleeding to death."

That's when I saw all the bright red blood running down Stephen's knee, and I felt so woozy I had to lie down on the grass until my head quit spinning. In fact, just remembering that makes me feel woozy again. I must be coming down with something.

Anyway, while I was lying down, Mother put Mecca ointment on Stephen's cuts and bandaged his leg and arm. Brian wanted to know how I was going to be a nurse if I faint at the sight of blood. I told him I wasn't fainting, that his arguing had made me dizzy, and if he hadn't argued with me, I would have been quite capable of taking care of Stephen. I did check Stephen's other leg and arm to make sure they weren't broken, until Mother told me to leave Stephen alone. Honestly! I was just trying to help. At least Stephen realized that. He said, "You're just like a real nurse, Bobby," while I was checking his leg and arm. Stephen is so sweet.

Monday, June 18, 1945

I saw the German prisoner! Here is how it happened:

The Veterans Guard soldier called to a nursing sister and told her he needed someone to wheel the prisoner to treatment. The nurse said she didn't have anyone available just then as it was a busy day, but then she caught sight of me and said I could do it. At first the guard didn't want me to, but she said it was me or no one—so it was me. I was scared to death. The prisoner was already in a wheelchair, so all I had to do was wheel him out of the hospital room.

I tried to act like I wheeled German prisoners up and down halls every day, so I said very crisply, "Which way, please?"

The guard said left, but I was so flustered, I went right. The guard had to chase after me. (And he was quite stout and elderly and very out of breath after a few steps. I don't know why the army had him guarding prisoners! Anyone could escape him easily!)

He yelled at me, "Don't you know your right from your left, young lady?"

I thought I'd die of embarrassment on the spot. My face was so hot you could have fried an egg on it! The German prisoner turned his head around and grinned at me. I thought he'd look like a monster, but he was about the same age as Alex, with light-brown hair and really nice green eyes, and very white teeth. Without thinking, I grinned back at him, then realized what I'd done and quickly frowned and stared straight ahead. I feel so bad for smiling back, especially after hearing Brent's story. I'm supposed to hate Germans, aren't I? This is all too confusing.

Tuesday, June 19, 1945

After our Geography exam today (which I think I did quite well on), a bunch of us went to the store at the corner for a cold pop. I was telling Betty and Lydia about the German prisoner at the hospital, and Rick Anderson said that he heard some girls had sent love letters to prisoners at a POW camp up north and the girls were arrested and taken to court! He said it all started when a prisoner smiled at one of the girls at a hockey game! Just like my prisoner did! I've committed the *heinous* crime of treason. I keep waiting for policemen to pound on the door. I'm so scared.

Got a letter from George. He said he had heard about the horrible things the Germans were doing and that was why he volunteered to fight—to stop those horrible things from happening.

Wednesday, June 20, 1945

Am at Aunt Lily's trying to distract myself with my garden. In the newspaper this morning I saw a photograph of some women in

Belgium who had their heads shaved by the people in their town after liberation, because they collaborated with the Germans. Mr. Preston at our school has a bald head (not because he collaborated, but just because nature did that) and he doesn't look too bad, but I think I would look dreadful without hair!

I'm afraid to go home in case the police come looking for me. I'll probably have to plan to escape if they do, because I don't think I could live in a prison. I wonder if anyone would come visit me there. My life will be forever tainted by one smile.

And speaking of prisoners, Nancy says her brother isn't doing too well. He doesn't like to be in the house very much, barely sleeps, and she can hear the front porch floor squeak all night long as he paces up and down. She is very worried about him.

My forget-me-nots are all gone except for the odd one here and there. I wonder if I'll be here next spring to see them, or in prison!

Thursday, June 21, 1945

I finally broke down and told Mother of my crime. "Is that why you've been *skulking* (good word from Mother so I'll use it) around here for two days?" she asked. Then she told me that when a person smiles at another person, you can't help but automatically smile back, and not to worry. I didn't divulge any vital war secrets. I have my suspicions Mother was really laughing at me, but I am very relieved.

Brian asked me what Nancy's favourite colour is. I told him it's yellow. I wonder why he wanted to know that?

YOUNG SPIES PAY PENALTY
Despite extreme youth, two Nazi boys paid with their lives for spying on allied troops in Germany.
—London Free Press, *June 18, 1945*

Friday, June 22, 1945

I was turning pages in the newspaper when I saw a small picture. It showed a boy being tied to a stake. He was seventeen years old! Like Brian! But the Allies were executing him, because he and his sixteen-year-old friend were members of the Hitler Youth Movement and were caught spying on the Allies. They were tried in a military court in France and sentenced to be shot! How could our side shoot two boys for spying? I showed it to Alex and asked him if it was true or maybe a hoax. He said it was true. I told him Brian would have been stupid enough to spy on the enemy if someone told him to, but they shouldn't shoot kids for being stupid. All kids are stupid at some time.

All Alex said is, "Terrible things happen in war."

Then I showed it to Mother. She said I should stop reading the newspaper. I told her I can't because I need to know what's going on. Maybe I should write the newspaper and tell them not to print upsetting pictures, but then, if it's true, I guess the pictures should be printed, even if they are upsetting. I wonder if everyone is as confused as I am?

Saturday, June 23, 1945

I got such a shock today. And I'm mad as a hatter! Heck, I'm mad as hell, as Dad would say. Here is what happened:

This afternoon there was a knock at the door. Brian just about fell over himself to open it. Nancy was there. I was quite delighted because I was pretty bored. Mother and Aunt Lily were having tea in the kitchen and I was studying for my Math exam on Monday. I elbowed Brian out of the way and invited Nancy in, but Brian didn't go away.

"I didn't know you were coming over," I said to Nancy.

Nancy's face got quite pink. "Actually, Brian invited me to go to the movies this afternoon."

Now I know what *flabbergasted* means, because that's what I was—FLABBERGASTED!

Brian looked all embarrassed and told me to scram. I watched them go down the sidewalk and Brian gave Nancy a yellow rose! A rose out of AUNT LILY'S GARDEN! A ROSE THAT I GREW! He made me a conspirator! I can't believe Nancy went to the pictures with stupid Brian. I'll give Brian a piece of my mind when he gets back!

When I went back in, I saw Aunt Lily and Mother looking very guilty as they sipped their tea. "You knew he was asking her to the pictures," I accused Mother. "Why didn't you tell me?"

Aunt Lily quickly said, "Why don't we go downtown and look at some material for your sundress, Bobby?"

So, even though I was very mad at everyone, and I wanted to say no, I agreed. Mother started to say that I should stay home and study, but suddenly said I could go, as long as I studied all evening. I guess she felt sorry for me.

I did get some pretty blue fabric, the exact same colour as my forget-me-nots. Aunt Lily kindly paid for it, which saved me a fair bit of my pay, but all I could think about was Brian and Nancy on a DATE! How could Brian do that to me? Nancy is MY friend!

Sunday, June 24, 1945

After church today was the Sunday School picnic at Springbank Park. Nancy spoke to me a couple of times, but I pretended I didn't hear or even see her. I helped with some of the little children's games, then Nancy asked me if I'd go in the three-legged race with her. I had to speak to her then because she asked me a direct question, but I kept my voice quite cold (hard to do on a hot, hot day) and said I had already promised Betty I'd be in it with her. I felt a pang in my chest when I saw

Nancy's face fall, but I hardened my heart by remembering she'd gone on a date with Brian. She'd betrayed me. As soon as she left, I quickly found Betty and asked her to be my partner for the three-legged race and she seemed quite happy to have been asked. Now I know why. Unfortunately, Betty isn't very good at the three-legged race. She's too worried about what she looks like when she runs, and she squeals a lot. We came in last.

Caroline put Billy in the Best Baby Contest, but he didn't win. Those judges must be blind! He was easily the most beautiful baby there.

Then Dad made himself sick. He bragged to Grandma that he could eat an entire brick of ice cream all by himself as he loves ice cream so much, so Grandma bought him his very own! Dad's eyes nearly fell out of his head when he saw the size of the brick, but Grandma was looking smug, so he ate the whole thing. Mother kept telling him to not be so silly, but he was determined. He finished it, but he spent the rest of the afternoon lying on a blanket under a tree moaning and clutching his stomach and embarrassing us all. It was a dumb picnic. Nowhere near as good as last year's.

Monday, June 25, 1945

Wrote my Math exam. Didn't work today because I needed to study for my Science exam tomorrow.

Tuesday, June 26, 1945

Alex's birthday today. Stephen and I put our money together and got him a new fountain pen. I remember when we used to send pens to him overseas so he could write letters home.

The only good news today is that I wrote my last exam, and Brian is going to a Reserve Army camp at the Thames Valley

Golf Course for two weeks starting July 1. He's bragging that he's going to live on rations, learn to shoot, and do night training. Too bad it doesn't last all summer. My life is miserable. I can't even be excited about school being over for two whole months. Summer is no fun without Nancy.

Wednesday, June 27, 1945

I changed my volunteer day from Sunday to Wednesday so it would be different from Nancy's. Mother says I'm being silly and to call Nancy and make up. I told her I was the one wronged here and Nancy should call me. "She's tried to," Mother said. "But you won't talk to her. You're as stubborn as your father."

I said, "I am NOT like Dad." That's when Dad walked in and said, "What's wrong with being like me?" I could have told him about the ice cream for a start, but I didn't because he looked tired.

Before I went to the hospital, I picked up my yearbook from school. It has a page of past students who have died while on active service. I'm so glad Alex is not on that page! So very glad. There were quite a few names on it, though, which made me feel very sad.

Thursday, June 28, 1945

We had a terrible storm early this morning. The loud pounding of the hail on the roof scared the life out of me. I thought someone was trying to break in. Stephen ran out in his pyjamas and collected some of the hailstones and put them in Mother's icebox for a snowball fight later. Mother let him because she said any bit of ice is a blessing these days as ice is scarce and the weather so warm.

Weeded the garden in the afternoon and told Caroline all

about Nancy and Brian. Caroline said you can't stop true love. I told her they've only gone out once. It can't be true love yet. Can it? The hail destroyed the last of my forget-me-nots. They have withered away, just like my friendship with Nancy. She has forgotten me.

Friday, June 29, 1945

I just read what I wrote yesterday and had a sudden *epiphany*. Of course it isn't true love. This is Brian! I give them one more date until Nancy sees what Brian is REALLY like—annoying, disgusting (he eats with his mouth open, for crying out loud), and sometimes he smells after playing football. Maybe she already feels that way after their first date! It won't be long before Nancy will be my friend again.

> *One thing in particular about their country* [England] *is the women—they do everything that a man can do and doing a swell job, too.*
>
> —Lawrence Haworth, June 1944

Saturday, June 30, 1945

Now that it is summer, I am to work every Saturday afternoon and every Monday afternoon. The hospital said there would be more help available once the men are back from overseas so they probably wouldn't need me in the fall, but I don't mind. At least I get to earn some money over the summer, and it's better than babysitting the two brats down the street. I guess no one knows I smiled at the German prisoner. He's gone away now. I wonder if he gets to go back home to Germany like our prisoners get to come home to Canada. I bet he hates that they lost the war. I know I hate losing anything.

More hospital coaches with our soldiers arrived today at the

C.N.R. station. Some of them fought at Dieppe and were captured and were prisoners of war. A few were in bad shape, and after hearing Brent's story I know why.

A girl followed a stretcher with a soldier on it. He was sleeping, but she was dabbing her eyes with a handkerchief. I asked her if he was her brother, but she said he was her husband. She looked too young to have a husband. She kept glancing down at the stretcher with horror. That's when I noticed he had a nasty, red scar stretching from his hair, down his right cheek, to under his chin. It looked quite awful, like someone had tried to cut his head in two. I asked her if she was going to faint, but she said she didn't think so. I don't think I'm ever going to be able to use the head-between-your-knees fainting treatment I read in the *A to Z Home Medical Book*.

Started cutting out my sundress this morning. Aunt Lily, Grandma, Caroline, and Mother helped, though Caroline didn't do much but run after Baby Billy. Finally Dad took Billy out to the garage. "Let's get you away from this hen party before they contaminate you," he said. "You need to be with the men."

Mind you, Aunt Lily didn't help with the cutting a lot either, as she is very upset because she's been told she'll have to leave her job in August when more of the men get back.

"They said we should put away our overalls and put our aprons back on," Aunt Lily fumed. "Aprons! Imagine! We do those jobs as well, if not better, than most men and with half the complaints. Now we're told all we're good for is the kitchen and having babies. We women were there when they needed us, and now they just want to throw us away."

That's when Mother took the scissors away from her because she was afraid Aunt Lily would cut my material to pieces in her anger.

"You could marry Sam," Caroline said. Then Caroline told

us Sam calls all the time and has even come to the house, but Aunt Lily won't speak to him.

"And be someone's domestic slave?" Aunt Lily said. "Have to check in with someone every time I want to leave the house? Marriage isn't for me."

Then Mother got mad and said she didn't feel like Dad's slave. And Caroline said she could hardly wait until James came home and they could be a proper married couple. Then Aunt Lily said, "Remember what Dorothy Dix says, that *women have changed in their relationship to men, but men stand pat just where Adam did when it comes to dealing with women.* Dorothy hit the nail on the head with that one. Men are never going to change. They want women in the kitchen and not using their brains and working!"

Aunt Lily said that now that she has had a taste of it, she likes her independence and her own money, and Grandma put in her two cents' worth and said it was unnatural for a woman not to want a husband and a baby. By then it was time for me to catch the bus for work. We never did get my dress entirely cut out because everyone talked so much. I'll finish it tomorrow.

Sunday, July 1, 1945

I'm in my room because Dad said he was tired of looking at my long face and to quit mooning around as I was ruining his radio program. He and Mother and Alex and Julia and Stephen are listening to a comedy show with Johnny Wayne and Frank Shuster. How my long face could ruin their program, I'm sure I don't know. It's just that today I should be volunteering with Nancy, but I'm not, and Brian and Nancy went out again last night, and Betty and Lydia weren't around so I had to stay in on a Saturday night. At least Brian went to his Cadet camp today, so I don't have to see him for two weeks!

I spent this afternoon writing George all about Nancy and Brian. I'm sure he'll agree with me that they are not suited for each other.

It's Dominion Day. At church this morning, Rev. Goddard said we should all be particularly thankful today that we have a free country. Brent was at church, but in the middle of the service he got up and left. Mrs. Rev. Goddard watched him leave and seemed quite anxious.

I sat with Mother and Dad, though I was supposed to work in the nursery today with Nancy. Why can't Nancy see how disgusting Brian is??? Of all the boys in the world, why does she have to go out with him?

Julia was just here. In my bedroom! She said that she understood that I felt hurt because Nancy was going out with Brian, because she had a similar experience with her best friend. In the end, though, she said it all worked out and they are best friends again. She said to just think that maybe Nancy might be my sister someday. That was supposed to comfort me? Nancy married to Brian??? I don't want things to work out. I want it just the way it was before. I will speak to Caroline tomorrow about getting a new girlfriend for Alex. Julia doesn't understand anything.

Monday, July 2, 1945

I walked the five blocks to Aunt Lily's to see Caroline and asked if she had any girlfriends who would be interested in Alex. She asked me what was wrong with Julia. I said, "She's too mousy for Alex. She's not a good influence on him. He shouldn't be working at a factory."

"Don't be so jealous," Caroline said. "You always did think Alex was your very own and now your nose is out of joint because you have to share him."

Before I could protest, we heard the mailbox *clunk* and there was a letter from James. Caroline tore open the envelope, all excited, but as she read her mouth rounded in a horrified O. Here is what happened:

She finished reading and stared at the wall a few minutes, then shoved Billy in my arms. "Take care of him. I have to go to see Mother," she said.

But I wasn't going to be left there all by myself while something exciting was happening, so I plopped Billy in his baby carriage and I trailed along behind her. Caroline went right to Mother and wrapped her arms around her and started to cry. All I could make out between sobs was the word "Australia."

Mother asked me to make a cup of tea for Caroline, and then they sat down. I plunked Billy on a blanket on the floor with some pots and lids for him to play with and filled up the kettle. It was hard to sort out what Caroline was saying, because she was gulping tears and tea all at the same time as trying to speak, but it seems that the Australian government is making arrangements for Caroline to take a ship to Australia to be with James.

Mother said, "Your father and I thought this might happen. Australia is James's home after all."

Then Caroline got mad and asked why they hadn't told her that before, and Mother just shook her head. "Dad didn't want to upset you."

Now I know what the secret fight was about! Mother wanted to tell Caroline and Dad didn't.

"Well, I'm not going halfway around the world to somewhere I don't even know!" Caroline said.

"You and James must have talked about his home," Mother said.

"We didn't do much talking," Caroline muttered.

I snickered and Mother raised her eyebrows at me. I suggested to Caroline that going to Australia might be adventurous and *exhilarating*.

She snarled at me, "You go then." And started wailing again.

I told Mother that Caroline was in the grips of female *hysteria* and a good slap across the face usually brought a person back to their senses.

Mother said it was time I went to work.

That girl was there visiting her husband with the scar. Her name is Irma. She cried all the way down the corridor after her visit.

Tuesday, July 3, 1945

Smallman and Ingram's Department Store has changed its name to Simpson's. Mother and I took Caroline to see the new store, hoping it would stop her crying. Dad is almost as upset as Caroline that she is to live in Australia. I think the reason he didn't tell her before is that he hoped maybe it wouldn't happen. Caroline was always his favourite, and he is pretty smitten with Baby Billy. Actually, we're all smitten with Baby Billy. Well, it might not happen because Caroline is quite adamant that she is not going to Australia.

I bought a pale-pink Tangee lipstick. Mother lets me wear lipstick now, but says it has to be a light colour suited for a young girl. I don't know why she still thinks of me as a YOUNG girl, when I have a job. I do love having some money to spend, though I've discovered that with movies, and Victory Stamps to put into my war saving booklet, and streetcar fare, my pay doesn't go too far! I'll have to do some babysitting to make more if I want to buy lipstick.

Mother bought a new girdle. I told her she should buy a second one for Dad's stomach. Mother tried to pretend she was outraged and told me not to be disrespectful, but she started to giggle just like Caroline and I were doing. Mother did make me promise not to repeat my comment to Dad.

Why don't men wear girdles? It seems to be fine for their stomachs to stick out, but not for a woman's. That doesn't seem fair.

Thursday, July 5, 1945

I got an invitation in the mail! In the mail! I can't stop looking at it because it is so pretty. Betty is having an end-of-school party tomorrow evening. She could have just telephoned, but a mailed invitation is much more elegant. If I ever have a party, I'll have mailed invitations.

It's to be a MIXED PARTY. That means boys and girls together. I don't know what to wear. I don't even have time to make my sundress, because the party is TOMORROW. At least I have a new lipstick.

Friday, July 6, 1945

Noon

Caroline is lending me a skirt and blouse. She would not lend me any stockings because she said she only has one good pair left and she's keeping them for whenever she sees James next—IN CANADA! She said it like that—in capitals. Even though the war is half won, nylon stockings are still scarce. In fact, most things are still rationed.

Aunt Lily gave me some of her Cinderella Leg Tan. It's like the makeup old women put on their faces, except it goes on your legs. It is supposed to make your legs look like you have stockings on, when you really don't.

I have the skirt and blouse on right now so I can admire myself. The skirt is full, and black with tiny white dots. The blouse is white. I think I look pretty good, especially when I swirl around and the full skirt flares out a bit. I'll have to remember to swirl at the party if I can.

57

Just kicked Stephen out of my room! He said, "You look all spotted, like you have the measles." Obviously Brian is rubbing off on him. I'll have to speak to Mother about that! Maybe there's another camp Brian can go to when he's done his Cadet camp.

I wonder if Nancy will be at the party?

Friday, July 6, 1945

11:30 p.m.

I haven't decided yet whether I had a good time or not, but here is what happened at the party:

When Dad dropped me off at Betty's double front doors, my stomach did a bunch of flip-flops. I'd never been to a mixed party before. I really wished Nancy was with me because I don't think I would have felt so nervous. But she wasn't, so I took a deep breath and went in. Betty's mother made a big fuss over my skirt and blouse, turning me this way and that, saying I looked "so adorable and grown up." Then she took me through to the backyard where the party was being held. I couldn't believe my eyes.

There were lanterns hanging from the trees and vases of flowers sprinkled across the lawn. A long table with a white cloth and a crystal punch bowl and glasses stood along one side of the yard. Everything looked so elegant, like something out of a Hollywood picture. I immediately thought that I should make our yard at home look like this, but then realized Stephen and Brian and their friends would just ruin it, and Dad would hate the lanterns.

There were a lot of kids at the party, but no one was talking, and for a mixed party, there wasn't any mixing. The boys were on one side of the lawn and the girls on the other. I went over to the girls' side.

Lydia said she really liked my skirt, but for one moment I

swear the Worm of Jealousy had struck Betty, because she frowned when she first saw me. But then she quickly squealed and said how wonderful I looked, and tucked her hand through my arm, so I might have been wrong. Then she said she had just the thing for that pimple on my chin, Burdock Blood Bitters, which cleans the blood and clears up pimples. I didn't even know I had a pimple! It must have come on awful fast as it wasn't there when I left home. I even looked in the mirror in Betty's washroom when I got a chance, but I couldn't find it! Just in case, though, I held my hand in front of my chin all night.

It was a dumb party at first, with the girls all pretending they didn't see the boys, even though they did, and the boys pretending they didn't see the girls, even though *they* did. The boys looked uncomfortable dressed up in their Sunday suits on a Friday evening, and I think all those lights and flowers and the table with the white cloth and the crystal punch bowl made everyone feel awkward.

Then Nancy arrived with her brother Brent. Later I found out he had just walked her down from their house, but Betty's mother insisted he had to stay for a bit. It's pretty hard to get away from Betty's mother when she insists. It really hurt to see Nancy and know she wasn't my friend any more. I thought maybe I should go and talk to her—but then, shouldn't she come over and talk to me? But she didn't.

Brent started to chat with the girls and some of the boys began to drift over to the girls' side. Then someone put on music and finally, we mixed. I even found a couple opportunities to swirl my skirt out when someone called my name and I had to turn around to see who it was. The party got fun after that.

Rick Anderson came over to talk to me. He said, "What's cooking?"

At first I thought he meant he could smell something frying

and I sniffed the air, but then I realized he was asking me what was happening, like they do in the pictures. I must admit he looked very handsome. I could tell that some of the girls were fighting the Worm of Jealousy because it was me he was talking to and not them. Rick said I looked swell and I thanked him politely, feeling quite adult at a mixed party. I did remember, though, to keep my hand over my chin. We talked a bit about the summer and he is going to help out at his father's garage. I told him about my hospital job and he seemed quite impressed.

As we talked, he kept stepping toward me, making me move backwards, until I realized he was heading me toward some bushes. Just as my back hit a branch, Brent came up with a glass of punch for me. Then I had two boys talking to me, though Brent is really a man. Still, I've never had two boys talking to me at once and it was very exciting. If I could have swirled my skirt, that would have made everything perfect! Rick kept looking at Brent, like he wanted Brent to leave, but Brent stayed, and eventually Rick said, "I'll see you around, Bobby," and left. "You be careful around that young man," Brent said. "I don't know him, but he looks like he might be trouble."

Trouble! I wonder if Rick was backing me up into the bushes so he could get me alone and kiss me! Rick might be a wolf!

Brent asked me if Nancy and I were having a fight, because he hadn't seen me around their house lately, and Nancy seemed unhappy. It was very embarrassing, Brent being Nancy's brother and all. I was mumbling about being busy at the hospital and my garden, when all of a sudden there was a huge *bang* and before I knew what happened, I found myself face down in a forsythia bush, Brent on top of me. Then I was being hauled up out of the bush by Rick and another boy from school, and Betty was shrieking hysterically, and Lydia was pulling leaves out of my hair. Brent scrambled to his feet and looked very upset.

Betty's mother came rushing over and Nancy came up and took Brent's arm. I told everyone I was fine. It seems Brent heard the bang and thought it was a bomb, so he threw us both into the bush. A truck had backfired on the street! I told him not to worry, that Alex had been very nervous of loud noises, too, when he came back from the war, so I was used to being thrown in bushes. I really wasn't, but I was trying to make him feel better. Brent was so terribly distressed that Nancy took him home. I really did feel quite bad then that Nancy and I weren't talking, as she looked as upset as Brent.

It should have been quite romantic having a boy save my life, except for the branches poking my back, my skirt thrown up around my thighs, and leaves in my hair! Gosh! I hope my underwear didn't show. I'm trying to remember which pair I had on, whether they were the blue ones with the holes in them or my good pink pair. Oh! Double Gosh! Everyone would have seen that I didn't have garters and stockings on! They'd know I'd used leg makeup! I'll never be able to show my face in public again!

Anyway, after things settled down, we had a nice outdoor supper, then Dad arrived to pick me up. Just as I was thanking Betty and her mother for a lovely time, Betty said, "It's too bad Brian wasn't able to come."

I told her Brian was away at Cadet camp. That's when I remembered Betty giving Brian the eye at the Victory celebrations, and I got a plan. A great plan. I'll write it out later, as I'm too tired now. I must remember to tell Mother *exactly* how I got green stains on Caroline's white blouse before she thinks the worst. I hope the stains come out or Caroline will be very mad. I must also remember to get some Burdock Blood Bitters. Still can't find the pimple, but it won't hurt to clean my blood.

Saturday, July 7, 1945

My legs are orange this morning! I can't believe it! Mother says it must be dye from the leg makeup. That's just swell! I have to go to work with orange legs!

> *The families of the psychotic or emotionally disturbed veteran and the physically wounded or crippled men require advice on how to receive, understand and treat the veteran at home.*
>
> —Toronto Daily Star, *September 30, 1944*

Saturday evening

Irma came to visit her soldier husband this afternoon, and he threw a lunch tray at her! It made a terrible clatter (which isn't a very good thing in a hospital where most of the patients have trouble with their nerves) and the dishes broke. What a mess, with food and china pieces all over the floor.

The nursing head went rushing in and brought a crying Irma out to me and told me to make a cup of tea. I took Irma into the nursing office and hurriedly put the kettle on to boil on the small burner, while Irma sobbed into a handkerchief. I made the tea and gave Irma a cup, then had a cup myself as I didn't know if I should leave her alone. After a while Irma stopped crying and began to talk to me.

She said she's from Ottawa but will stay in London until her husband is better and can come home. Irma's a real lady. Even while upset, she still holds her teacup with her little finger pointed out! Then Irma asked if I knew a boarding house she could stay at as the hotel is quite expensive and the YWCA is full of factory girls. I immediately thought about Aunt Lily's house. Even with Caroline and Billy there, Aunt Lily has an extra bedroom, and Caroline might be leaving soon if she decides to go to Australia. I told Irma I might know of a place and I'd see her on Monday. She smiled really sweetly at me and thanked me and called me "Nurse." I had to tell her I wasn't a nurse, but that I was going to be one.

She's quite beautiful—like a movie star, with black, tousled curls, really wide grey eyes, and perfectly smooth skin. I hadn't realized how beautiful she was before, as I mostly see her with tear-splotched cheeks.

I made myself a nurse's hat out of paper and pinned it to my head and looked at myself in the mirror. It looked dandy. But there was a knock on the door and I raced to answer it, hoping it was Nancy come to make up. It was Brent. He came to apologize for throwing me in the bushes last night. I told him it was fine. As he was leaving he asked me if I knew I had a piece of paper stuck on my head.

Sunday, July 8, 1945

Mother and I went to hear a missionary speak at church this evening. The missionary talked about her work in Africa teaching people to read. She said they are very short of missionaries to do vocational and medical work and to preach the Gospel in China, India, and Korea. I wrote George that along with devoting my life to nursing, I have decided to also devote it to being a missionary. Gosh, I really miss George. Letter writing is fine, but I wish I could see him. But as Grandma says, if wishes were horses . . . well, I can't remember the rest. Maybe you get a horse ranch or something.

Aunt Lily wants to meet Irma.

Monday, July 9, 1945

Along with my medical book, I have now started to read the Bible to get a jump on being a missionary. It makes for a lot of hard work. I finished all about the beautiful Garden of Eden and am at the generations of Adam. Adam was nine hundred and thirty years old when he died! That's what the Bible says, so it must be true, but I wonder if the years back then were shorter than ours are now. Maybe a year back then was just a couple months. Dad just turned fifty and his hair is already all grey and he's getting bald at the front, and Grandma is ancient at seventy-three. At nine hundred and thirty years old, I bet Adam didn't have a hair on his head, and had more wrinkles than even Grandma.

I just realized that if I'm going to be a missionary, I will have to forgive people. But I don't want to forgive Brian for taking Nancy away from me. I'll guess I'll just be a nurse. I don't really mind because between reading the Bible and my medical book, I don't have much time to do anything else. Also, the Bible is pretty boring. I must remember to tell George I'm back to being only a nurse again.

My garden is looking swell these days. We've had just the right amount of sun and rain, and my radishes and lettuce really came up. I'll have to weed it tonight.

Monday, July 9, 1945

After work

When I got home from work, Mother said Rick Anderson had telephoned for me. "Please tell him not to call between seven and eight in the evening, Bobby," she said. "I don't want our neighbours to think we're not patriotic." (We're not supposed to use the telephone between seven and eight o'clock at night so we don't tie up the lines when soldiers want to call their families.)

Anyway, I telephoned Rick back and he asked me to go to the beach at Port Stanley with him on Thursday, as he has the day off work. He said his mother and sister will be going, too.

It took some convincing, but Mother finally said I could go. I reminded her that the hospital said I was very mature. "I just don't like you going off somewhere with a boy," she said.

"It's not just somewhere," I said. "It's the beach, and his mother and sister are going."

Before bed

In all my excitement, I forgot about George!!! I had to get out of bed to ask Mother if it was appropriate for me to go to the beach with Rick when George said he was taking me on a date when I was sixteen. She said it was just fine as George and I aren't dating or going steady or anything. Omigosh! I need a new bathing suit! I wonder why Mother is letting me date when I'm not sixteen yet? Well, I'm certainly not going to ask her.

Tuesday, July 10, 1945

I got a wonderful bathing suit! Aunt Lily took me downtown to Simpson's and I got a bathing suit for $5.95. That was pretty expensive, but Aunt Lily paid half of it, and Mother gave me some of the "Baby Bonus" money she got for me, and I added some of my wages to make up the cost.

As of the first of this month, the government pays Mother a Family Allowance for each of us children at home. Mother says it is to help out with expenses because children are costly to raise. Dad says all it will do is encourage people to have more babies, and cost him more in taxes! Mother told him to simmer down before he gave himself a stroke.

The bathing suit is blue and white and in two pieces. The top fastens at the back and has two shoulder straps and the bottom is a short skirt. My stomach shows a little in between the two pieces. Grandma said that's *scandalous* and Dad didn't look too pleased, either, but Mother said it flattered me (I think she said that to make Grandma mad, but I'll take it as a compliment), and Caroline and even Julia like it.

And while Aunt Lily and I were shopping, Mother finished my sundress! She said she only had to pick out one or two of the seams I'd put in. I wish Nancy and I were friends so I could show her my bathing suit and sundress.

Aunt Lily and I also met Irma downtown for lunch today. It was very civilized (unlike meals around our house! Stephen is taking up right where Brian left off and Mother is fit to be tied). Irma is so dainty and pretty. I want to be just like her. I remembered to put my napkin on my lap and I stuck my little finger out when I lifted my water glass, because I wasn't sure if that little finger applied only to teacups. Aunt Lily was very taken with Irma and they made an arrangement for Irma to come and see Aunt Lily's house.

Wednesday, July 11, 1945

More mail today—my report card. I passed everything, even Math, with surprisingly good grades. In fact, the school said I stood third in the entire grade-nine class! Mother says she is very proud of me. I'm now in grade ten.

And yet more mail. Got a letter from George. He says he doesn't see a problem with Brian and Nancy dating. He says Nancy can still be my best friend and date Brian, and Nancy and I should make up because everyone needs a best friend. Obviously he needs to be here to appreciate the *dilemma* I'm in.

I volunteered at the hospital today. Irma didn't come as she went to Aunt Lily's to see about staying there. Have to go and borrow Dad's razor and shave my legs before I go to the beach tomorrow.

Thursday, July 12, 1945

Late evening—burned to a crisp (sunburned, that is)

I went to the beach today with Rick and his mother and little sister, Emily. I had a wonderful time. Here is what happened:

We took the train down to Port Stanley on Lake Erie. I wore my sundress over my bathing suit. Rick's mother said she really liked my dress. She was very nice. Emily is three years old and quite sweet. Rick and I sat together on the train. It was hot, hot, hot, so we opened one of the windows on the train, though it didn't help much. I did enjoy watching the trees slip by, and as I sat in the aisle seat I also got a chance to admire Rick's wavy hair when I looked out the window.

The day started out grey, but the sky cleared up completely on our way to the lake. We walked right to the beach when we got to Port Stanley. It was wonderful. The water was so blue I couldn't tell where it ended and the sky began. We sat on a towel and talked for a bit, then we went swimming, except, I don't really know how to swim, so I just paddled around in the shallow water and played with Emily. After that we went to Mackie's Restaurant and got some french fries and orange drink, even though Mrs. Anderson had packed a nice picnic lunch of ham sandwiches, with pickles and onions. (I picked my onions off. I didn't want onion breath if I talked to Rick.)

Mrs. Anderson and Emily had a nap after lunch, so Rick and I walked down the beach and looked at the Port Stanley Ballroom. It costs fifty cents to dance. It would be so romantic to dance there, next to the beach.

Then we wandered onto the pier, and that is when it happened! Rick kissed me! All my life I imagined what a real kiss with a boy would be like. I think it would have been better if Rick had picked the onions off HIS sandwich. It was very *pungent*. (I looked that word up in my dictionary right now.) I tried to not breathe through my nose, but discovered that if you don't breathe through your nose, and someone else's mouth is over yours, there's no way to breathe at all! I felt like a fish gulping air between kisses. Soon it was time to take the train back.

Rick walked me home and held my hand all the way. I kept hoping Betty or Lydia or anybody I knew would see me with a boy holding my hand, but we didn't run into a single person. It might be because it was beginning to thunderstorm.

At the door, I told Rick I had a very nice time and quickly went in before another onion kiss. I must admit, while the date was lots of fun, the kissing was a tiny bit disappointing. I wonder if all kisses are so sloppy. Our lips kept slipping off each other, though it didn't seem to bother Rick at all, so maybe it's just me.

(Mother said Dad was roaring mad when he went to shave this morning and his razor was dull, and to ask next time before I shave my legs.)

Friday, July 13, 1945

I'm so sunburned today from the beach that Mother said I was to sit in the shade so I didn't get sunstroke. Stephen and I did go and pick beans from my garden for supper early in the morning before it was too hot. I can't believe how many beans are on one plant! Mother says we'll can them. I thought I might write my letter to George today instead of Sunday because I can't do much else. I wrote two letters. In one, I told him about the beach and Rick, and in the other I didn't. I threw both letters away. That's when I decided to switch to writing in here and to save the letter for later. I'll ask Caroline what I should say in the letter.

Later

I went to see Caroline, but she was too crabby to talk to me. She only thinks about herself and moving to Australia. Alex just got home from work. Maybe I'll ask him.

Even Later

I knew Alex would help. He said I should just tell George that I went to the beach with a school chum named Rick and Rick's family and tell him about the water and the ballroom and the pier. I asked Alex if he'd kissed girls overseas at the war. He smiled and said, "Mind your own beeswax, kiddo." He almost sounded like my old Alex right then.

I think it's a very good idea of the government's in training the lads that come back to a trade or occupation and pay them while they learn. I shall certainly take advantage of it when I get back.

—*Lawrence Haworth, June 1944*

Saturday, July 14, 1945

At the hospital today, there was a leaflet I picked up for Alex called "Back to Civil Life." I also picked up a couple leaflets about how the government will pay for veterans to go back to school, called "Training and Education—Doorways to Opportunity," and gave them to him. The government would pay his school fees, plus he could receive sixty dollars a month living expenses. I gave them to him at supper and told him I thought he should leave the factory and go back to school and get a better job. Dad was a little put out and said, "What's wrong with the factory? It's good honest work," and Mother glared at me. I felt bad as I didn't mean the factory wasn't a good job. I certainly didn't mean to hurt Dad's feelings. I told him I was sorry.

Irma was at the hospital this afternoon. She is going to board with Aunt Lily until her husband is better. His name is John. He was very nasty to her today and wouldn't take a newspaper she had brought him, but threw it on the floor. Poor Irma.

Sunday, July 15, 1945

Before I went to church, I asked Alex if he was going to leave the factory and go back to school and he said no. I said, "What about the 'Doorways to Opportunity'?" and he said he didn't want to go through them right now. I asked him why not and he said the factory suited him. I told him he could get a better job with more education, and didn't he want to be a newspaper man?

That's when Mother said, "Stop badgering Alex, Bobby."

I don't understand why Alex doesn't want to do more with his life. He's supposed to be all better from his shell shock now. Or at least that's what the hospital said.

Wrote George about going to the beach with a chum, like Alex said, and all about Julia. And Irma. And Alex. And that Brian came back from Cadet camp today and the first thing he did was telephone Nancy! I had hoped that while he was away, she might think twice about dating him, but I guess she didn't as Brian plans to see her this evening.

Everyone around here has baseball fever. All they do is listen to baseball on the radio and talk about Yankees and Pirates! It's very dull.

Monday, July 16, 1945

Irma moved in with Aunt Lily today. Aunt Lily is happy to have her as a boarder because she says it will be a bit of money coming in for when she's tossed out of the factory. I'm so glad Irma is living there as I can visit her any time I want and learn to be a lady.

Irma says she and her husband were only married three months and then he went overseas. He was there for two years. She says he used to be so cheerful all the time, but now he's moody and irritable. She says the doctors at the hospital say he has had a nervous breakdown. I told her about Alex's battle fatigue and how he is better now. I didn't tell her, though, how he wouldn't leave the factory.

I feel very bad for her. She's twenty years old, like Caroline. Irma really does have the most beautiful grey eyes, wide and rimmed with dark lashes. I wish my eyes were wider. Mine are sort of squinty. And an ordinary brown. I can't change the colour of my eyes, but maybe if I hold them wide open for a couple of days, I can stretch them.

I have been handed a piece of paper this week to fill out for this '39–'43 star or ribbon for being in CMF and don't think as I deserve it.

—*Lawrence Haworth, June 1944*

Tuesday, July 17, 1945

At breakfast Brian asked if I was practising to be an owl. He's such a moron. I asked him if he was going to another Cadet camp soon. No change in my eye size.

I went with Betty and Lydia downtown to a big parade the city put on to honour returning soldiers. I wanted to wear my slacks, but Grandma came over just before I left and said only loose girls wear slacks in public. I told her lots of women wear slacks now. Mother said I was right, lots of women do wear slacks, especially if they work in factories, but perhaps I should put on a skirt to wear downtown. So rather than argue, I wore a skirt. Grandma and Mother are so old-fashioned!

The soldiers were in trucks driving down Dundas Street. All the light posts on the side of the street were decorated with red-blue-and-white flags. There were great crowds and everyone was cheering and waving the Union Jack. I yelled myself hoarse. Some stores had signs over their doors saying "Welcome Home To Our Boys." Lots of people have signs on their homes, too, that say the same thing. I asked Mother if we could put a sign on our door. Alex overheard and said, "No," quite loudly. I asked why not and he said, "I didn't exactly come home a hero, did I?" and he left.

Mother's face was quite sad as she watched him go, but all she said was she thought it best not to put out a sign as it wouldn't be very sensitive to Aunt Lily's feelings, as Uncle Billy didn't come home.

I wonder what Alex meant. I think he's a hero. He even got some medals from the war, and only heroes have medals!

Betty asked me how Brian was getting along, and that reminded me of my plan. I better put it into effect.

Wednesday, July 18, 1945

I walked Irma home to Aunt Lily's after I volunteered at the hospital, and Aunt Lily invited me to stay for supper. There was a very interesting conversation at the supper table—you'd certainly never hear anything like it at OUR house.

Irma said she met a woman on the train to London who told her that she—this woman—had given her soldier husband permission to find a woman overseas if he needed to, because he'd be away from her for so long and she understood that men have needs. (It took me a while to figure out what *needs* she meant, as I didn't want to ask and seem childish!) This woman said that as long as he didn't fall in love with another woman, it was fine with her. Caroline said, "Well, I certainly wouldn't give James permission for any such thing! If I can go without, so can he."

All three of them were smoking after supper and Irma

offered me a cigarette. Aunt Lily looked like she was going to say no, but then she shrugged and said, "Oh, go ahead." I was delighted and felt quite grown up until I nearly choked to death when I breathed in the smoke. Caroline had to smack me on the back a number of times until I could catch my breath! It tasted dreadful. I don't know how anyone can enjoy smoking. But I held on to it anyway and took small puffs. I should borrow one from Aunt Lily and light it up in front of Betty and Lydia. Mind you, I'd have to learn to not choke first, and hold it properly so the ash doesn't fall on my skirt (I just noticed a hole!). Maybe I won't smoke after all. I feel quite ill at the moment.

Anyway, back to Irma's story. It turned out the woman's husband had an entire second family over in England! And he just upped and left them when the war was over and came back to Canada, and expected to start up where he'd left off with his Canadian family. The woman found out about all this when his OTHER WIFE wrote him. Irma said the woman's husband had been shot in the thigh, and the woman told Irma she wished it had been a little higher. It also took me a few minutes to figure THAT out!

Then Aunt Lily said that maybe the woman was so eager to give her husband permission because of what she, the woman herself, was doing at home. "What's good for the gander is good for the goose," she said. She said some men were coming home to children that couldn't possibly be theirs, but most were ignoring that fact to keep the peace and get on with their lives.

Then Caroline started to talk about James and Australia—the only topic of conversation she knows any more. That's when I took Irma around my garden. She said the border of alyssum and lobelia I planted was wonderfully fragrant. I told her all about the forget-me-nots and showed her the leaves. It is too bad there aren't any more blooms. I also told her about the love-lies-bleeding that came up last year (though there is none this year) and how Aunt Lily tore them to shreds because she thought they had killed Uncle Billy. Irma dabbed her eyes and said she was so lucky that John came back to her alive.

Mother just came in my room and asked me why it smells so strongly of cigarette smoke. I told her it was because Aunt Lily, Caroline, and Irma were smoking and it got in my hair. I didn't see any reason to tell her about me smoking, as I don't plan to ever again. I'm going to visit Aunt Lily's house tomorrow. I think I'm going to learn a lot there.

I gave up holding my eyes wide. It was giving me a headache. I'll just have to live with squinty eyes.

Hundred of Londoners flocked to the C.N.R. and C.P.R. stations at noon today to welcome a group of war brides and their children.

—London Free Press, *June 18, 1945*

Thursday, July 19, 1945

Our house is in turmoil! Caroline got a letter today from the Australian government saying that she has to be ready at a moment's notice to travel to Australia. (Well, a few weeks' notice, really.) We thought she would go in September. She cried and cried and told Mother she wasn't going. Finally, Mother told her that was enough tears. She said quite firmly, "You married James and you are his wife. He deserves to have his wife and child with him."

"But what if I hate it there?" Caroline said. "I'm sure I'll hate it. What if his family are horrible? What if they don't like me?"

"You make them like you. If anyone asks you how you like Australia," Mother said, "you smile and tell them you love it. That way you'll make friends quickly. And James's family can't help but like you. James's mother has already sent you a couple of lovely letters and she sounds very nice. You're a married woman now, Caroline, with responsibilities, and James will be there to help you. And you love him, don't you?"

Caroline nodded, then hugged Mother and said, "I'm going to miss you and Dad so much." Then Caroline hugged me and said, "And I'll miss you, Bobby, and all your hare-brained ways." I'm not sure if that was meant to be complimentary or not.

Mother said that we would all miss her, but we would write each other every week, and she said that soon Caroline would find herself so busy with her husband and Billy and her new life, she'd probably not even have time to be homesick.

So it looks like Caroline is going to Australia. Now that she's decided to go, Mother says there are a million things to be done, and she'll need me to help with the meals. At least I can make fish-and-potato casserole in white sauce now—with chives, of course. I offered to show Caroline how to make my casserole. She said no thanks, even though I pointed out to her that Dorothy Dix says, "It is hunger for home-cooking that drives more men into matrimony than any other thing." Caroline said I believe the most ridiculous things, but I bet once she thinks about it, she'll want to learn how to make my casserole.

A letter arrived from George. He said that I could be any-thing I put my mind to—a nurse or a missionary or anything. He said my day at the beach sounded dandy and that there isn't much opportunity to go to a lake in Saskatchewan. School is out right now for him, too, so he is back home at his family's farm. He said he's surprised how much he can do to help with only one arm. He also said he has heard stories simi-lar to Brent's, and war changes everyone it touches, but that I was right and some people don't show their ghosts as much as others, who prefer to keep them hidden. I think George him-self is one of those who keeps his hidden for the most part, though at times I think I saw them in his eyes.

Evening

Just heard on the radio that there were huge explosions in Halifax! They must have thought they were under attack, though Japan is a long way from Nova Scotia. It was the Navy armament depot blowing up.

Dad is pretty upset that Caroline is leaving. He spent the evening puttering around in the garage. Mother said to leave him alone for a bit.

Friday, July 20, 1945

I was invited to Betty's for supper. It was sort of boring. All Betty does is talk about her clothes and her shoes and her jewellery and boys who like her. I read her *Screen Stars* magazine while she talked and occasionally nodded so Betty would think I was listening. But I'll just have to put up with her, because I need Betty for my plan to work.

The movie stars in the magazine are beautiful and they go to parties all the time and drink champagne. They probably never have to do dishes or listen to their brothers burp. It must be a glamorous life.

Supper was very nice, with crystal and china and thick linen napkins, but oddly the Worm of Jealousy didn't turn even once. I can remember when that Worm twisted so much when I saw all the nice things Betty had that I thought I'd throw up.

But even though supper was elegant, I must admit that meals at Nancy's are much more fun, with everyone talking over each other and even sometimes yelling until Rev. Goddard tells them to be quiet, which doesn't last very long. But I guess that is never meant to be for me again. Unless, of course, my plan works.

Betty asked me to go to the show tomorrow afternoon, but I

told her I had to work at the hospital. Betty's father then asked me all about my job on Mondays and Saturdays. I told him I also volunteered on Wednesday afternoons.

"You should be doing that," he said to Betty.

Betty's mother was horrified and said that Betty couldn't possibly associate with strange men, as "she has delicate sensibilities."

"Stuff and nonsense," Betty's father said. "A dose of hard work would knock some common sense into the girl. She's been drifting around all summer like dandelion fluff." (I really like that description of Betty.) "And it doesn't seem to be hurting Roberta at all. She's turned into a fine young woman." (Let me be crystal clear: Betty's father said that.)

So Betty is coming with me Wednesday to sign up to volunteer. Spending time with Betty will help with my plan.

Here is my plan: Betty really likes Brian. I decided if I throw the two of them together often enough, they will like each other and then Brian will transfer his affections from Nancy to Betty. I don't care if he goes out with Betty.

Saturday, July 21, 1945

Rick called and asked me to go to the movies with him tonight and—surprise of surprises—Mother said I could go! I asked Rick twice if he was sure he wanted to go to the show WITH me, and not just see me there. (Like last time when I thought I had a date with him to go to the movies and was so embarrassed to find out I didn't!) He assured me he wanted to go WITH me. So I think I got it straight this time. It is a proper date.

I told Brian that Betty is going to volunteer at the hospital and tried to build her up to make her seem like a selfless saint. I also told him how pretty she is, and how many clothes she has. He looked at me like I'd lost my mind. But at least I put my plan into action. He's thinking of her, I just know it.

July 21, 1945

Evening

It was a real date! Rick came by the house and met Mother and Dad. Mother told him I had to be home by eleven at the latest. She is so embarrassing, treating me like a child. Dad grunted a hello, then went back to reading his paper. Rick must think I have the most dreadful family.

We walked to Loews Theatre and saw Judy Garland and Robert Walker in *The Clock*. Except I didn't really see too much of the movie! Here is what happened:

At the movie theatre, there were some kids from school waiting in line who normally don't talk much to me, but because I was with Rick, they all came over and we chatted. I was so happy to be on a real date. The girls were very nice to me and said how much they liked my blouse. (I got it from Caroline. She is passing some of her clothes on to me because she can't take them all with her, so I'm looking very stylish these days.)

I was in seventh heaven. I tried to pretend that I go on dates all the time, and yawned a few times to show I was bored, until one of the girls asked me if I was tired.

Inside the theatre I wasn't sure whether or not to have popcorn when Rick asked if I wanted some, because I didn't want to be the type of girl who spends all of a boy's money. I very politely said no, even though I love popcorn. Rick didn't get any either. It was very exciting when he took my hand and led me into the theatre and we sat down. (I'm so glad I put some of my Etiquette deodorant on my hands. I figured if it stopped me perspiring under my arms, it should work for my hands. And it did. My palm was only a bit sweaty, but Rick didn't seem to notice.)

We sat and watched the newsreel, and when the picture started, Rick put his arm around my shoulders. I tried to watch the show but all I could think about was Rick's arm around my shoulders. Then he kissed me! Right in the picture show! I took a quick look around and I saw some other kids from school were kissing too. Rick kissed me again, and as he kissed me I felt his arm start to come down *my* arm. I knew exactly where his hand was heading! I suddenly remembered Dorothy Dix warning girls about going to movies with an amorous youth and to stick them with a hatpin if they got too fresh. But I didn't have a hatpin so I whispered, "Don't be fresh," and moved away.

"Miss Prim and Proper," Rick said, and he laughed and didn't seem mad, but after a few minutes he started to kiss me again.

I wonder if everyone kisses so sloppy. Rick puts his lips completely over my mine and I feel like he is trying to swallow my face. It's quite hard to breathe. I always feel like I want to dry my face with a handkerchief when he stops, but I don't because it might be rude.

I did get quite a start, though, when I felt his tongue. I kept my teeth shut tight together after that in case his tongue accidentally slipped into my mouth again. I'm not sure who to ask about kissing. Certainly not Betty. Nancy would probably know. Maybe Caroline, or Aunt Lily and Irma. So Rick kept kissing me for the entire show, which was a shame as I missed the picture and I wanted to see it.

One of the best moments, though, was after the show. We were coming out when one of Rick's friends came up and said, "Do you and your girlfriend want to come to get some ice cream?" GIRLFRIEND! I didn't even know I was a girlfriend. I guess that means I have a boyfriend!

I had a chocolate ice cream cone. When we sat down in a booth, Rick elbowed my side and pointed at Mr. Lee, who was scooping out the ice cream. "He's a Jap, you know?"

I've known Mr. Lee all my life, but I never realized he was Japanese. He's just the nice ice cream man who occasionally gives me two scoops instead of one as a treat.

"I bet he's a spy," one of the girls whispered. And the others all nodded.

"He should be in one of those camps they send Japs to," another boy said.

I asked what camps was he talking about, and he said all the Japs on the west coast were sent inland to live in camps that were guarded by military police until the war was over because the government thought they might be spies for Japan. I was quite surprised to hear that. "Do you mean like concentration camps?" I didn't like to think Canada had concentration camps like the Germans.

"No," Rick said. "They're different."

"How?" I asked.

"I don't know," he said. "They just are."

Then I asked, how did the government know they were all spies? The other boy said they didn't know they were all spies, but they put them in the camps just in case they were.

"Even the children?" I asked.

"Of course! They're Japs too."

"Kids can't be spies," I said. "That's ridiculous."

And Rick said, "You're a smart one, aren't you, Baby-face, always asking questions."

I don't know if he meant that remark to be a compliment or not, though he did call me "Baby-face." But I can't imagine all of the Japanese people in Canada would be spies! And why would they want Japan to take over Canada? I expect they left Japan and came to Canada because they didn't like it there in the first place.

"Baby-face." I guess that's Rick's nickname for me. I wonder what I should call him. Mother calls Dad "Sweetheart," and Dad calls Mother "Darling," but I don't think any of those *endearments* are suitable for Rick. I'd feel silly calling him those. Maybe I should call him "Honey"?

Can I be Rick's girlfriend and also be George's friend? I guess so, because it's not like George or I ever dated or anything. Still, it feels a bit strange.

Sunday, July 22, 1945

Nancy's brother Brent wasn't in church. Maybe he's sick. Nancy sat with her mother and sister. I really miss sitting with her. I wonder if she misses me? Stephen says the three Goddard boys he plays with are visiting their grandmother in Toronto for a few days to give Mrs. Rev. Goddard a rest. Their grandmother will be the one needing the rest after they visit!

Stephen and I were picking yet more beans from my garden when Caroline came out and flopped in a lawn chair. "Thank goodness Billy's asleep," she said. "He's so fussy these days. It's going to be a long trip with him teething."

Irma joined us after a bit, though she was going to see her husband John at the hospital later that afternoon. This seemed like a perfect opportunity to ask them both some personal questions.

I gave all the beans to Stephen and told him to take the basket home to Mother. After he left, I pretended to check my tomatoes while I got up the courage to ask Caroline and Irma about kissing. I described Rick's kissing (though I didn't say it was Rick—I said it was a friend's boyfriend) and how SHE SAID it felt slippery and sloppy, and Caroline laughed. "Sounds like your new boyfriend is a lousy kisser."

I pointed out to her again that it wasn't *my* date! I didn't want her to think that the only boy I could get was a lousy kisser. I don't think either of them believed me because Caroline said, "Don't you let a boy do anything you don't want him to do. You be careful."

Then Irma said I had to realize that boys were going to be all over me. "Boys like what you have, Bobby, and you have it amply."

I was completely mystified as to what on earth she was talking about. That is when Caroline said, "Don't be such a dope, Bobby. She means you're very well developed—well endowed—and boys really like that."

I must have still looked puzzled because Caroline leaned forward and whispered, "Your chest, you ninny. Boys like big chests on girls!"

I was so embarrassed I went right home.

I just looked at myself in the mirror and she's right. I do have a large chest, bigger than hers or Mother's. Mother says I take after Dad's side of the family in "that respect." Unfortunately Grandma Harrison is dead so I can't tell if I take after her or not. Now that I think about it, I do remember her chest hung quite low, almost to her waist. I hope I don't keep growing and that happens!! Maybe if I wear my brassiere at night it will stop me growing. I just realized how funny that sounds—growing. It's like I'm a tomato or bean plant in my garden.

Evening

I am *infuriated* with Caroline! She told Mother about Rick and me kissing! Mother came in to my bedroom a few minutes ago to have a little "talk" and asked me if I remembered her telling me where babies come from. I wanted the floor to open up and swallow me, I was so embarrassed. Mind you, Mother's face was as red as mine. Who does Caroline think she is? Miss Know-it-all. Miss Prude. Especially after she and James made Billy BEFORE THEY WERE MARRIED!!!

I didn't write George today because I didn't know what to say about going to the show with Rick. It is the first time I haven't written a Sunday letter to him. Maybe I'll ask Irma if I should have a boyfriend and still write to George. I certainly won't ask Miss Tell-All Caroline!

I asked Mother about Mr. Lee. She says he is Chinese, not Japanese, so I guess he can't be a spy.

Monday, July 23, 1945

Morning

Now Mother's told Aunt Lily about Rick and me, because Aunt Lily also warned me about boys! Honestly! My whole life is known by the entire world! At least I found out why Mother let me go on a date. I overheard her tell Aunt Lily that it wouldn't hurt me to know other boys besides George, especially when I was so young. Then Aunt Lily said, "She's going to be a popular one with the boys."

"I know," Mother said. "But I can't keep her locked up in her room."

I knew what they were talking about. I had no idea everyone was so interested in my chest!

Aunt Lily's not too happy these days as she no longer has a job. The night shift was discontinued at the aircraft factory last week and she was let go. She said it was a good thing Irma was renting a room, otherwise she'd have no income other than her widow's pension. Dad is very worried that the factory will close down entirely as they are not making very many parts for airplanes any more, just for the Mosquito aircraft. He says the bosses have assured the workers that it won't close entirely, but he says he doesn't believe them. He says they'll do what's good for them and to heck with the workers (though he didn't say "heck"). I hope it doesn't close because he and Alex will both be out of work and we might starve.

Tuesday, July 24, 1945

I've invited Betty to supper. I told Mother I had to return the invitation. She said that was fine, but I have to help make the meal, and also I need to help her clean up the house before Betty comes as Mother has been busy packing for Caroline. I said, "How much more stuff does Caroline need to pack, for crying out loud?" Mother told me not to use slang around the house.

All I know is that Caroline will sink the ship with all her suitcases and trunks! Anyway, it is a small price to pay if my plan works and Nancy is my friend again.

Dad came down this morning rubbing his chest and complaining of pain. I told him he had indigestion. He said, "I wish like hell someone would take that damn medical book away from you." Mother asked him to please watch his language. I told Mother that indigestion could also cause irritability. It's a good thing I'm not reading the Bible any more. I barely have time to read my medical book these days.

Evening

Betty came to supper tonight. She looked very pretty in a green skirt and white-and-pink-striped blouse. I sat her between Brian and me. She asked Brian all about Cadet camp and she hung on his every word like everything he said was incredibly fascinating. I think she's as good an actress as Judy Garland because I found everything Brian said to be very, very boring. Who cares what rations he ate?

I sang Betty's praises until everyone looked at me like I was crazy, even Betty. But then Brian started talking about Nancy's brother, Brent, and Betty started pouting because no one was paying her any attention. I kicked her shin to alert her to the fact she was sulking, but all she did was yelp and her bottom lip stuck out even farther.

It seems Brent wants to go to Japan and fight. Brian says he's very restless at home and can't settle to anything. Rev. and Mrs. Goddard are horribly anxious that he might sign up. We've heard some awful stories of how badly our soldiers are treated in the Japanese prisoner of war camps and Brent's already been in the German POW camps. Nancy must be very worried. Alex says he doubts the military will let Brent go as he was a POW in Germany.

Brian also said he heard that Japanese women were fighting right alongside the men. The Japan war is supposed to be going pretty good for us now, but Dad says you can't believe everything the newspapers say. (Which is a strange thing for Dad to say because he is always reading the newspapers out loud to Mother!)

After supper I had Brian play cards with Betty and me. Betty kept tossing back her hair and laughed at everything Brian said. Then Brian and I walked Betty home. On the way back I asked Brian if he thought Betty was nice. He said, "I guess she's all right. A bit empty upstairs, though."

I must make Betty appear smarter so Brian will like her.

There's a new serial in the newspaper called *Airman's Wife* by Renée Shann. I read it to Caroline while she bathed Billy before bed. We both think it is quite romantic.

Wednesday, July 25, 1945

Betty started her first day volunteering. She's actually not bad because she spent a lot of time talking to the men, and laughing with them. It really surprises me because I remember when I went to the hospital for the first time to visit Alex I wouldn't look at or talk to any of the men. I thought they would look horrible with scars and missing legs and things. It doesn't seem to bother Betty one bit. One of the other volunteers said to me, "I wish she'd stop flipping her hair and come help us with these drinks." But the men seemed to like her and were quite cheery when we left.

I brought Betty home for supper again. I just ate a bit of supper to make up for Betty's share, because I didn't want us to run out of food if we're going to be poor. I'm pretty hungry now, though.

I told Brian about how good Betty is with the veterans at the hospital. Later, after Betty went home, I told Brian that Betty really likes him and said she'd like to go out with him some time. She didn't actually say that, but I know she does want to go on a date with Brian. Brian just shrugged. He's so annoying. Betty is very pretty, why wouldn't he want to go out with her? I was annoyed, I told Brian he should do something about his halitosis!

Thursday, July 26, 1945

I don't understand what is wrong with my family! Alex doesn't want to get a better job or a better girlfriend. The war is over, yet he doesn't seem very happy about it. Brian doesn't seem all that interested in Betty even though she is twice as pretty as Nancy. Caroline can only think about Australia. Dad grumbles around the house and drinks baking soda for his indigestion and Mother keeps wanting to have little "talks" with me.

A letter came from George. He said to tell Irma that her husband isn't mad at her, he's mad at the world because of what happened to him, but Irma is the one who is handy, so he'll be mad at her.

George says that is how he felt when he first lost his arm. I feel really bad that I didn't write George a letter last week. I just can't seem to think of anything to say.

Friday, July 27, 1945

A perfectly horrible day. I am going to throttle Stephen! Here is what happened:

The Goddard boys were here today playing with Stephen (back from their grandmother's, who is probably *prostrate* with grief that they've gone!—that's a sarcastic remark). When I walked into the kitchen where the three of them and Stephen were all having a snack, one slapped the other and said, "Don't be fresh!"

Another one said, "You're a sloppy kisser!"

And the third one said, "If I had wide eyes, I'd be beautiful," and he batted his eyelashes.

That's when it hit me. Stephen had read my diary to them! To the Goddard boys! Just writing that makes me SO MAD all over again.

I screamed at Stephen and started to chase him around the table. A chair got knocked over with a huge *bang,* which brought Mother into the kitchen, yelling, "What the sam hill is going on here, Bobby?"

Yelling AT ME! I'm the one who was wronged and she yelled at me! She said I was older and should know better than to race around the house. I told her Stephen had read my diary to the Goddard kids. She said they weren't goats so I shouldn't call them kids! What that has to do with anything, I'm sure I don't know! Obviously, she doesn't even care that they read my PERSONAL diary.

Stephen is hiding from me right now, but I'll find him, and when I do . . .

I wonder how he found the key to the box I keep my diary in? It's hidden inside a small tear in my pillow.

> *Friday evening—in my bedroom—away from my*
> *horrible family—because Mother made me, but I don't*
> *care. I'd rather be here by myself than with them anyway.*

Mother made Stephen apologize to me and promise to never read my diary again. He got off very lightly, compared to MY punishment. It's so unfair.

Here is what happened:

At supper everyone snickered as I again told Mother how awful it was that Stephen read my diary to the Goddard boys. I asked Stephen how he got inside the box where I keep my diary and he said, "Oh, that was easy, Brian told me you keep everything hidden inside your pillow where it's ripped."

I couldn't believe it. "How did you know that?" I demanded of Brian.

"You threw your pillow at me once and the key fell out. Later on I found the hole in your pillow where you keep all your special secrets!"

"That's just swell," I said. "Now everybody in the whole wide world knows all my business!"

Mother told Brian and Stephen they weren't ever to go into my room again, but I saw Dad trying not to laugh. Even Alex grinned, which pierced me to my soul, as I thought he, at least, would be on my side. I told Mother I would take my supper into my bedroom to eat in privacy, even though no one respects mine. She said I would have my supper at the kitchen table with the rest of the family. I started to cry, which furthered my misery.

That's when Julia said, "Don't worry, Bobby, no one will remember all this tomorrow," which turned my misery to anger that not one single person in this place understood how hurt I was, so I said to her, "Why are you always here? Don't you ever eat supper at your own house?"

Mother's faced was *suffused* with crimson she was so mad, and she ordered me to my bedroom without any supper, even though Julia said, "She's just upset, Mrs. Harrison."

I don't want Julia sticking up for me!

Mother was just in and said she was ashamed of my behaviour and that I was to apologize to Julia. I told her I didn't think Julia was very good for Alex, and she said, "What on earth do you mean? Julia's a perfectly lovely girl."

I told her that I had given Alex the flyers for veterans' education and how he didn't want to use them and I thought it was Julia who didn't want him to have any ambition. And then she told me it wasn't for me to say who or what was good for Alex, that it was his decision. She also said I was to stop pushing Betty at Brian at every opportunity, because everyone knew what I was doing, and it was time I made up with Nancy and stopped moping about the house. The same house, she went on to say, that I was to get up early and clean from top to bottom tomorrow as punishment before I go to work. I think I'll ask Aunt Lily if I can live with her.

Even later

My bedroom is like Grand Central Station tonight! People just come and go in here as they please. Alex was just in and he is very mad at me for hurting Julia's feelings. I feel really bad that Alex is mad at me, worse than the fact that Mother is angry with me. He used to be my best friend and now he hates me.

> *There are a lot of people, particularly over there* [Canada]
> *that do not think what it is like to lose all their life's work*
> *and building of a home in less than a second . . .*
> —*Lawrence Haworth*

Saturday, July 28, 1945

Another horrid day. My life is miserable. I dusted and swept and washed floors at home all morning, and then I had to go to work at the hospital. I'll probably come down with lockjaw or lumbago from sheer exhaustion, and not one single person in my family will care. I bet if I died, none of them would even notice I was gone.

A bomber (United States' own) ran into the eighty-second floor of the Empire State Building in New York. It was foggy out at the time and the pilot lost his bearings. Thirteen people were killed. I bet the people in New York thought they were being attacked by the enemy, not their own airplanes!

I apologized to Julia this evening. She said she remembered what a mixed-up time it was to be my age, but not to worry as everything would turn out fine. I doubt that very much.

Sunday, July 29, 1945

A very boring day. I didn't feel like going to church so I told Mother I was coming down with mumps. My neck did look a little swollen this morning when I checked in the mirror so it wasn't a complete lie. She said I looked fine to her and to get dressed for church. Geez! Dad was tired and didn't want to go to church, and Mother let *him* stay home!

Then I had to stay dressed up all day because Rev. Goddard was coming to do his church visit in the afternoon. I told Mother that Rev. Goddard had seen me in my nightgown before, and he wouldn't care if I was in my Sunday dress or not! I wanted to wear my slacks.

"Well, then, you just go and put on your nightgown and you can wear that while we have tea with the minister, Bobby," Mother said.

That's when Dad said I was to stop backtalking Mother all the time, because I was giving him a sour stomach. I could have said something about where his sour stomach came from (he eats a fair amount), but I thought perhaps I'd said too much already and didn't want to push my luck. I didn't wear my nightgown. I kept on my dress.

Rev. Goddard said he was sorry I hadn't been visiting them lately, then exchanged significant glances with Mother. I quickly told Mother I would make the tea and I fled to the kitchen and hid out there so I wouldn't have to talk about Nancy.

Went to work in my garden in the evening. There are scads of beans. Stephen came to help me pick them. I wanted to haughtily tell him to go away, but I needed the help, plus he said, "I didn't mean to read your diary. I'm really, really sorry." I forgave him because I could tell he meant it. Stephen is quite sweet on his own. I think it is those Goddard boys who make him so *rambunctious*.

Mother says we will put the beans down for the winter. I'm glad because if Dad does lose his job, at least we'll have beans to eat. I also have lots of green tomatoes, which will soon be red tomatoes, and we can have beans and tomatoes to eat all winter.

I met Brent on the way home from Aunt Lily's. He was out for a walk, he said, because his house is too noisy at times. I told him I knew what he meant as our house is noisy too. He asked me how Alex is doing, and before I knew it I was telling him all about Alex having battle fatigue and being in the hospital, and not wanting a better job and not wanting a "Welcome Home" sign on our house and that he doesn't think he's a hero. I don't know why I told Brent all that. Maybe because I don't know what to do to make Alex feel like a hero, and I was hoping Brent could help because he was over at the war too.

Before he went, Brent said I should make up my quarrel with Nancy and that she really misses me. I wanted to rush right over and tell her I miss her, too, but I didn't know how to.

I wonder if Brent feels like a hero. I didn't think to ask.

Monday, July 30, 1945

I forgot to write George yesterday. I'll do it later, as Rick invited me out for a walk this evening! Must get to work at the hospital.

Evening

Rick and I went for a long walk near the river. It was very nice, except the part where Rick kept wanting to kiss me all the time. We sat on the grass and watched the water slide by, and Rick kept putting an arm around me. I decided to distract him by talking so he could see I was smart along with having a large chest. I asked him what he thought about the Warsaw Ghetto and wasn't it horrible what the Nazis had done there. He looked at me like I was crazy, but at least it stopped him kissing me. "What's the Warsaw Ghetto?" he asked.

So I told him all about how the Nazis crowded all the Jewish people in Warsaw, Poland, into a slum area and how they wouldn't let them leave or give them any food and how many of them died of cold and starvation. (I heard about this from some of the men at the hospital and read more about it in the newspaper.)

A number of the Jewish people in the ghetto started to fight the Nazis. I told him I thought that was very brave because they didn't have hardly any weapons. The Jewish people lost and were put on cattle cars and shipped off to the murder camps.

That's when Rick said it was time to head back home. He didn't seem very happy. Maybe boys don't like it when girls talk. Maybe they don't like girls having brains because it makes them, the boys, feel dumb. Maybe all boys just want to kiss all the time. Now I'm worried that Rick will go off me. It's nice to have a boyfriend. Everyone talks to you like you're special, and Betty and Lydia are very jealous. I even like pretending that I'm sorry I can't go with them to the movies because I'm with Rick, when I'm not really sorry at all. I better not talk to him any more or he won't want to be my boyfriend. Mind you, George didn't seem to mind my talking. I really like George, but he is so far away and Rick is right here. If it wasn't for dumb old Brian, Nancy and I would still be friends and I could talk to her. I have so many questions. I should write a letter to Dorothy Dix.

Tuesday, July 31, 1945

I overheard Mother and Aunt Lily talking yesterday. Mother said she regrets now that she let me start dating so young. Aunt Lily said not to worry, as I was a smart girl and I wouldn't let anyone take advantage of me. It was nice to hear Aunt Lily has every confidence in me, but I don't feel that smart sometimes, especially when Rick calls me "Baby-face" and my legs go all weak.

Got a letter from George. He says he missed getting my letter last week, but maybe it was held up in the mail. I'll write him tomorrow. George says I shouldn't push Alex, that Alex will figure out in time what is best for him. The trouble is that I don't think Alex *can* figure out what is best for him, but I know I can.

Mother, Aunt Lily, and I put down green and yellow beans all afternoon and evening! My face is steaming more than the canning pot!

Wednesday, August 1, 1945

Summer is half over! Mother and I are having a goodbye tea for Caroline next Sunday in case she goes to Australia sooner than September. I've never been a hostess for a party before, so I'm quite excited. I think I'll wear white gloves. Unfortunately, I don't have time to mail out invitations, which would have been much more elegant, but I'll hand-write them and leave them in people's mailboxes tomorrow morning. I guess that's the next best thing to a mailed invitation.

Mother says I have to invite Nancy and her two little sisters, and Mrs. Rev. Goddard, and also Julia and her mother. I'm not sure what I'll say to Nancy. Maybe she'll want to make up with me and she'll tell me how sorry she is that she hurt my feelings, and that she will never go out with Brian again.

Grandma, Mother, Aunt Lily, and Irma are baking fruitcake for the tea. Irma has become like one of the family. Maybe I could ask her about George and Rick.

I chopped so many cherries and nuts and dates that I'll chop them in my sleep tonight.

Grandma and Aunt Lily were arguing again about Aunt Lily getting married and having children. Aunt Lily said she enjoyed just being an aunt. Irma said she'd like children someday, but then her eyes filled up with tears, and Mother gave her a big hug and told her these things have a way of working out in the end. Then Mother said that I could plan the table setting for the tea. Irma came with me into the dining room and we decided to push the table back to the wall, use white linens, Mother's good silver, Grandma's good china, and pick white and pink roses from Aunt Lily's garden and put them in vases down the middle of the table. It is going to look beautiful!

Then Irma and I left for the hospital. I had to do my volunteer work and Irma was going to visit John. On the way in the bus, I told her what George had said in his letter, that John wasn't mad at her, but at the unfairness of life, and she said that was all well and fine, but she didn't know how much more of John's surliness she could take. She said she was at her wits' end. She said she hadn't planned on having an ill husband to look after for the rest of her life. "I'm too young."

I remember the head nurse saying once that the mothers who came to the hospital to see their injured sons were so delighted to have them back that they didn't care what condition they were in, whereas sweethearts and wives looked at it quite differently. They looked to their husbands to provide for them, not the other way around.

I never did get a chance to ask Irma about Rick and George.

Betty volunteered again today. Her father drove her to the hospital. She said he is so proud of her, he raised her allowance fifty cents! She says she finds volunteering very fulfilling. I think what she really likes is all the attention. She doesn't work all that much, and spends most of her time chatting with the boys. I will say, though, that she is very good at putting them in high spirits, and the nurses say that is as important as serving drinks.

Evening

Caroline got a letter from James's parents. They said they can hardly wait until she and their grandson come to Australia, and that they have fixed up a little house for "the new family" behind their own house. It seems James helps his parents run a huge cattle ranch in the middle of Australia. Their nearest neighbour is a hundred miles away! Caroline is very upset. I told her maybe she'd see a real kangaroo. She said all she was going to see was dirt and in-laws and cows! She's terrified.

I just read all about my ovaries in the medical book. I wish I hadn't as it makes me feel quite woozy knowing all those different parts are inside of me.

Thursday, August 2, 1945

Got a letter from George. He said he guessed I must be really busy with my job, as he didn't get a letter from me last week either. He signed it, "Forget-me-not, George." I feel really bad, but I don't know what to say in a letter to him. I haven't heard from Rick in a couple days. Ever since I told him about the Warsaw Ghetto. I knew I shouldn't have talked so much.

I bought a Charmette Permanent Wave set. I could only afford the twenty-five curls for 69 cents. Fifty curls costs $1.15. I didn't have that much money to spend as I have to buy Caroline a gift for going away. I didn't tell Mother I bought the permanent, because she has a lot on her mind right now. Betty is going to do it for me tomorrow while her mother is out at a church meeting.

Gosh! Rick just dropped by the house and asked if I would like to go to the young people's dance at the church Saturday night. I'm so excited! If I can't have dimples or wide eyes, at least I'll have beautiful hair.

Brent came over and sat outside in the backyard with Alex this evening. They didn't appear to talk much, but sat there and smoked. I wanted to go out and join them but Mother said I should leave them alone.

Just read about pregnancy. On top of the ovary reading I did yesterday, well, I wish I had been born a boy! I had no idea having a baby was so disgusting. I'm surprised Mother had us as she likes everything around the house to be neat and tidy.

Still reading the newspaper serial to Caroline while she gets Billy ready for bed. I love Aunt Lily and Irma, but it's really nice when it's just Caroline and me. Like old times when we shared a bedroom. Mind you, I remember how mad she would get if I borrowed her perfume!

Friday, August 3, 1945

I will never show my face again! I might have to leave town altogether. Maybe I could go with Caroline to Australia. I'm wearing my winter hat on my head right now. I don't know what Mother will say. Here is what happened:

I went over to Betty's right after lunch. Lydia was there too. I sat in a chair in the kitchen and Betty put a towel around my shoulders. We opened the permanent, which smelled to high heaven, making tears run down our eyes! Betty rolled my hair in curlers and daubed the solution onto them, while I held my nose. Lydia tried to read the instructions to her, but Betty told her there was no need for that as she had seen her mother have her hair permed about a million times and knew exactly what to do. So Lydia went and made tea for us. I felt quite important having Betty working on my hair and Lydia making me tea. Like a movie star.

Betty started to ask me questions about Rick and did he kiss me and stuff like that. It was so nice being the one asked questions for a change that I think I might have divulged too much. I was feeling so worldly, with my hair being permed and having a boyfriend and all, that I told them that Rick wanted to kiss me all the time. I hope they don't tell anyone about that. I still haven't completely forgiven Betty for telling everyone I liked Rick in grade eight when I swore her to secrecy! She still says she didn't tell anyone about that, but I don't believe her. I made them cross their hearts this time as extra protection, but I still don't feel completely certain they won't tell anyone. Loose lips do more than sink ships. It doesn't take much to get a reputation as a loose girl. Like Cindy Garbaldi. Cindy Garbaldi is sixteen and the talk of our school. She wears really tight tops (now that I think of it, she and I are about the same size in that department) and bright-red lipstick. Boys' eyes nearly fall out of their heads when they ogle her. All the kids say she kisses any boy who asks her, and once she kissed the entire athletic squad on a dare!

Anyway, Betty finished curling my hair and put a towel over my head. We sat and read *Star* magazines about all the Hollywood movie stars, and talked for the afternoon. Lydia did point out that the permanent instructions said it should only be on my hair for forty-five minutes, but Betty and I decided to leave it curled for a couple of hours so I'd get my money's worth. Finally, Betty took all the curlers out. It was horribly curly, but she told me not to worry, it was always like that at first, and once she'd rinsed and styled it I would look wonderful. So we rinsed it, and it still stayed curly—in fact, it got worse!!! Betty couldn't even get a comb through it! Lydia tried to flatten it with her hands while Betty wet it down. At first we thought that had worked, but when it dried, the curl all came back. That's when Lydia said, "Maybe we should have taken the curlers out after forty-five minutes."

I made Betty lend me a hat to wear home despite it being close to ninety degrees out!

Mother just called me to come to supper.

Evening . . . late

I asked Mother if I could eat supper in my room, but she said I was to come and eat my supper at the table like everyone else. I just realized as I wrote that, that I could have told Mother I had my period and she might have let me eat in my room.

So I went to the supper table in my hat. Alex asked me why I had a hat on. I said, "Because I'm cold."

Mother said that I was being ridiculous and to take the hat off immediately.

When Dad saw my hair he then proceeded to ruin yet another meal by spluttering mashed potatoes the complete length of the table. I suggested to Mother that perhaps, after this, Dad should sit at the side rather than at the head of the table because then only the person across from him would have a ruined meal, rather than all of us.

Stephen complained, "I don't want to eat Dad's mashed potatoes. I want my own."

So Mother scraped everyone's mashed potatoes off their plates, the entire time blaming me for wasting good food! I think she should blame Dad.

I asked everyone what I could do with my hair, but Aunt Lily said that I would have to live with it until the permanent wore off. Mother said it served me right for not asking her before I used it. I am never leaving my bedroom again until my hair looks better. I will grow old and die in here.

Saturday, August 4, 1945

Morning

Stephen is a hero! I can't believe it! He's being honoured by the police department and everything. He and the Goddard boys were riding their bicycles yesterday just outside the city when they noticed a tree had fallen over the railway tracks. Stephen had the idea of taking off his red shirt and tying it to a post to warn the train, then they ran quickly to a farmhouse and told the farmer, who called the police. Stephen never told us a thing about it until the police and a photographer from the newspaper came to the house this morning. The policeman said Stephen was a very quick-thinking young man and a hero. Dad is fit to bursting he's so proud, but Stephen is quite shy about all the attention. I wish it had been me. I would love to be a hero and have my picture taken—but not with this hair.

Mother refused to call the hospital and say I was sick and couldn't come to work. She said I'd done this to myself and I had to live with it. "Pride goeth before a fall," she said. I have no idea what she's talking about. All I know is I have to go to work this afternoon looking like a circus clown. I wish I was already a nurse so I could wear a cap! Golly! I just remembered the dance! I can't go to the dance looking like THIS!

Night

I had a thoroughly miserable time at the dance. Here is what happened:

When I got home from work, Aunt Lily, Mother, Caroline,

Julia, and Irma tried to straighten my hair. They used oil, water, lemon juice, but nothing worked. They seemed to find it very funny, though I certainly did not. Julia told me the curls would grow looser with time. Finally Irma said she had a lovely hat I could wear to the dance.

When Rick came for me he asked, "Why are you wearing a hat?"

I said quite airily, "Because it's a *church* dance, silly. Everyone wears hats to church dances."

But when we got there, I was the only one with a hat on. People giggled and pointed at me, and Rick told me to take the hat off. I said I couldn't because I was in a church hall and I pretended I didn't care that everyone was laughing, though I felt like crying. I didn't know which was worse, the hat or my hair.

Betty and Lydia came over, and Betty said, "Oh, is your hair still a mess?"

And Rick asked, "What's wrong with your hair?"

Betty said, "She tried to perm it, but it didn't work!"

I was so shocked when Betty didn't confess that *she'd* permed it, that I couldn't find my tongue, and by the time I did, Betty had left.

Then Nancy came over and said that I looked very smart and she wished she'd thought to wear a hat, too. I thanked her and wanted with all my heart for her to be my best friend again. I wanted to tell her that, but I couldn't think how, and then Rick grabbed my hand and pulled me on to the dance floor and I never got a chance to talk to her the rest of the evening.

We only danced a couple times and then Rick said it was a dumb dance and wanted to go home. I think he was embarrassed to be seen with me. I bet he never calls me again.

Sunday, August 5, 1945

I feel utterly *forlorn* today. I also got my period. It's always the way. Just when I think life cannot get any worse—it does. Today is Caroline's going-away tea. I wore Brian's winter toque all night. It was quite hot for sleeping, but I think my hair is flatter. Mother is calling me to get ready for church. At least I can wear my hat there and no one will giggle.

Evening

I'm worn out, but the tea went very well. I told Mother we should put it in the society column of the newspaper. She said that would be fine if we were society, but we aren't.

Here is what happened:

I decided to not wear a hat at the tea, though many of the ladies did. I figured by now everyone had heard about my hair. When she arrived, Mrs. Turner said I looked wonderful with my new hairdo! "I wish I was younger," she said, "so I could try a new hairdo like that, but I'd probably give Mr. Turner a heart attack if I changed my hair now." I always thought she was a scary old woman, but she's really quite nice.

The entire house was full of women. Alex and Brian went off somewhere together, and Dad took Stephen, the Goddard boys, and Baby Billy fishing. He grabbed Billy's hand and yelled in the middle of the tea, "Let's head for the hill, boys, or these here women will take us over."

Mother said, "Henry, stop it. You're a bad influence on that child."

Dad just looked sad, and Mother put her hand on his arm. I know what they were thinking, that pretty soon Dad won't be an influence on Baby Billy at all when Caroline goes to Australia.

"Watch him all the time, Dad. Don't let him fall in the water!" Caroline said.

"That's what we're taking the fishing rods for," Dad called back. "To fish Billy out if he falls in."

That really didn't reassure Caroline at all.

A whole bunch of Caroline's friends from her old office came. Two or three of them were quite suitable to be Alex's girlfriend, but I couldn't very well ask them if they were looking for a boyfriend with Julia right there! Nancy and her mother and sisters came, but I was so busy, I wasn't able to talk to her.

Caroline's cheeks were pink with excitement and I could have stood there all day looking at her, she was so gorgeous. It's easy to see who got the beauty in this family . . . but I haven't figured out yet who got the brains. I suppose Alex—certainly not Brian.

The women brought many lovely gifts for Caroline, which was nice as she never did have a wedding shower, or even a real wedding for that matter. She got a lot of towels and linens (more for Mother to pack), and all the girls from the office got together and gave her a black, silky nightgown. Grandma said, "That will never keep her warm in that heathen place," and one of the girls said, "It's not supposed to keep her warm. That's James's job. This is to remind him of that." And they all giggled. I can hardly wait until I'm older and I can make jokes like that too. It was my job to write down the name of the person and the gift they brought Caroline, so she can send thank-you notes later.

Everyone said Mother and Aunt Lily had outdone themselves on the treats, and the fruitcakes were wonderfully light. Mother made sure they knew that Irma and I had helped. (I still have red stains on my fingers from those cherries to prove it, but seeing Caroline so happy made it all worthwhile.)

Irma is so nice. Many of the women commented on our table setting, including Betty's mother, who said the roses down the middle looked lovely and she wished she had a green thumb to grow beautiful flowers. Irma had arranged them, but she told everyone it was my idea. Irma feels like part of our family now. I greatly admire her manners and *fortitude*. She goes to see John most every day, despite his treating her so badly. I wish he would stop.

I never poured so many cups of tea in my life as I did this afternoon! At one point Mother sent me to Aunt Lily's to get more tea as we ran out! Caroline was quite weepy when everyone said goodbye. They all promised to write, which, if they do, means Caroline will be spending a lot of time replying. Caroline never did like writing letters. Having the tea party makes me realize she really is leaving. I'm going to miss her terribly. Just thinking about it now is making me cry.

Mother's calling me to come help clean up. All those cups and saucers have to be washed. Before I go, here is the big news! Sam was waiting outside to walk Aunt Lily home.

Monday, August 6, 1945

Every day there are more and more pictures in the newspaper of men arriving home from overseas. Pretty soon they are all going to be home. This is causing a bit of a problem because the women are mad that they have to give up their jobs so men can have them. At the hospital today, one soldier said he wouldn't want a wife who knew more about wrenches and ratchets than he did. He wanted one who knew how to cook and clean! I couldn't help myself, and said that women could do a lot more than cook and clean. He laughed and said I was a *suffragette*. I couldn't say I wasn't until I got home and looked up the word. It means "a woman advocate of a woman's right to vote." I guess he means I'm a fighting woman. I like that—a fighting woman.

Good news. Brian has decided to help on a farm for the rest of the summer to earn some money.

TERRIFIC NEW ATOM BOMB
SHAKES MORALE OF JAPAN
—London Free Press, *August 7, 1945*

Einstein's theory of relativity came out of the laboratory and into democracy's arsenal to help shorten the war with Japan.

—London Free Press, *August 7, 1945*

Tuesday, August 7, 1945

The Americans dropped a new, huge bomb on the city of Hiroshima in Japan yesterday. It's called an Atom bomb. The newspaper said it caused a great deal of devastation. There was an explanation as to what it is, but I didn't bother to read it as that's too much like Science class. Dad says that is a good thing as he doesn't like to think of Caroline travelling to Australia if the war is still on with Japan. Maybe now it will be over.

And speaking of Dad, Mother wants him to go to the doctor for his indigestion. He said, "Why, when I have my own nurse right here?" and he pointed to me.

Mother should know by now that Dad will never go to the doctor unless he's dying. He's afraid of them.

I brought Dad some bicarbonate of soda for his stomach. Mother wasn't too happy, but she knows there's no talking to Dad once his mind is made up.

*Sixty percent of Hiroshima was reduced to rubble and ashes
and life was almost wiped out by a single bomb.*
—London Free Press, *August 8, 1945*

August 8, 1945

The newspaper showed pictures of Hiroshima and there is
nothing left standing except the odd tree, stripped of any
leaves. Everything is coated in dust or ash. It looks like how I
imagine the end of the world would look. There were no pictures of any Japanese people. I wonder what happened to
them? The newspaper didn't say.

The Americans have asked Japan to surrender. Japan hasn't
replied.

Russia also declared war on Japan today. Dad says that fig-
ures, as Stalin, Russia's leader, sees a good thing happening
and wants in on it so he can share the spoils of war.

The new bomb was all the talk of the hospital today. Irma,
Betty, and I took the bus home together. Betty talked all about
the boys at the hospital and how she likes volunteering there.

When Betty got off at her stop, Irma told me that John
wasn't mean today, but he never talked to her once, just to the
other soldiers. That's when I said, without even thinking
about it, that maybe he was trying to make her not love him
any more so she'd leave him. I didn't quite understand what I
meant myself, but Irma went very quiet and then said, "I
think you might have hit the nail on the head, Bobby. Well, if
he thinks I'm that easy to get rid of, he's got another think
coming." Then she squeezed my hand and said, "You're so
smart, Bobby. What would I do without you?" That made me
feel very good, especially as I don't think of myself as really all
that brainy.

Thursday, August 9, 1945

Late night

The Americans dropped a second Atom bomb on Japan, this time on the city of Nagasaki. Dad heard it on the late news on the radio.

Friday, August 10, 1945

The newspaper today said that sixty thousand people were killed in Hiroshima. I've felt sick all day. I wanted to talk to Mother, but she's busy with Caroline, so finally I spoke to Alex after supper. I told him I can't begin to imagine that many people dying at one time and he said he couldn't either. Then I told him that when I was little, Grandma Harrison once told me that when someone dies, God hears that person's cry. I asked him what he thinks happens when sixty thousand people die at once. He said he didn't know, that there were too many things he didn't know about war. I told him I thought it must sound like a huge scream to God's ears . . . like the entire universe screaming, and he said it's not just God's ears that hear the screams, but every thinking man and woman's. He said it was the screams ringing in his ears that drove him over the edge in Italy.

That is the most Alex has ever spoken to me about his experience in the war. It helps me to understand a bit about how he feels, and I think I know what he means. I hear the screams too. I probably shouldn't be having so much sympathy for the Japanese, as they are at war with us, but part of me does.

I wish I could think of some way to help Alex. I feel so useless these days. I used my diary when he was in the hospital and I think that helped him get a bit better, but I don't think my diary will work this time. I've been racking my brain trying to think of some way to help him.

Got a letter from George. He says if I don't want to write any more he understands, but could I let him know. I'm so ashamed of myself, but I've left it so long, I don't know what to say.

I worked today as Mother wants me to go to the Mary Hastings Housewife Picnic with her tomorrow.

Things were hectic at the hospital this afternoon as more and more men arrived from overseas. The nurses are run off their feet. One asked me to hold a pan while she and the handsome doctor with the crinkly blond hair changed a dressing on a man's back. Looking at the blood-stained rag in the pan made me feel quite woozy, so I stared at the ceiling. The only problem was that when I went to walk out of the room, I couldn't see where I was going because I had my eyes turned upward, and I walked into the wall instead of out the door. I did, though, see the doctor grin at the nurse. I wonder if all nurses get woozy at first?

The greater parts of two great Japanese cities lie in complete ruin as the result of only two atomic bombing raids.
—London Free Press, *August 11, 1945*

Saturday, August 11, 1945
Morning

I wish Japan would surrender! I don't want the United States dropping another bomb on them. It turns out that Canada supplied the uranium to make the bomb. It was all done in secret.

My hair is finally a bit flatter. I wish I hadn't written that. Sometimes I think I'm not a very nice person when I can worry about my hair when sixty thousand people are dead and thousands more wounded.

Saturday, August 11, 1945

Late at night

A busy day. I thought the Mary Hastings Housewife Picnic would be dumb, but it was interesting. Grandma and Mother and I took the streetcar to Springbank Park. There was a huge tent set up at the pavilion. The place was packed with hundreds of women and some came quite a distance to be there. I had no idea so many women read the Mary Hastings Housewife column. Many of them were penpals who had never met each other until today. You would hear a squeal and a laugh and know that someone had met her penpal.

It was very hot and sunny, but there was free ice cream for everyone. The Girl Guides were taking care of the smaller children. I wonder why I never became a Girl Guide. The uniforms are rather nice.

There was a lovely display of sewing crafts, including a "Little Dutch Girl" raffle quilt. I thought it quite adorable. Mother and Grandma bought a couple of raffle tickets on it. I wonder if they'll win.

In the evening Rick and I went to see *The Valley of Decision* with Greer Garson and Gregory Peck at Loews. It was lovely and cool inside because they have a cooled-air system. I could have sat in there for a week.

While I was getting ready to go, I overhead Dad tell Mother that he thought I was going out too much with "that boy." Mother said I had a sensible head on my shoulders, and that it was only for the summer and once school started I'd not have time to go out to movies. I didn't know Mother thought I had a sensible head on my shoulders. She never tells *me* that.

I'm surprised Rick is still asking me out. After the dance, I thought I'd never hear from him again. He called while I was out at the picnic. I had a bit of trouble in the show when he put his arm around me and his hand wandered toward my chest. I half turned in my seat so he couldn't reach anything important and put my arm across my chest. Rick asked why I was squirming around so much. I told him I was just trying to get comfortable. By the end of the show, I felt like I had been at a war myself! Between fighting to save my *virtue* and the kissing, sometimes I think I'd rather go to the show with Betty and Lydia. At least that way I'd get to see the picture!

Sunday, August 12, 1945

I invited Betty over for the afternoon. I was showing her the clothes Caroline has passed on to me. She said she wished she had a sister to give her hand-me-downs as she only gets new things.

Afterwards we sat out in the backyard and drank lemonade. I invited Brian, *enticing* him with raspberry tarts. I was wishing we had a nicer backyard, without the horrible old garage, and the ground torn up by Stephen and his friends, and Dad's vegetable garden. I remembered how Betty's mother had their backyard all decorated with lights and flowers.

At least I had Mother's best glasses, and her white linen napkins. I tried to sit straight like Irma with my feet tucked under the chair and I stuck my little finger out while I sipped lemonade. I told Betty all about how Brian was working in the harvest. Betty said she thought he was wonderful and brave. Brian said, "What's so brave about chopping hay?"

After Betty left, Brian told me he thought her the silliest girl he'd ever known.

"But she's pretty," I said.

"Who cares what she looks like—she has empty air between her ears. Nancy has a lot more brains. Betty acts like she doesn't have a thought in her head."

I told him not to be so rude as Betty was my best friend. He told me I was being stupid not having Nancy as a best friend any more, because she was smart and funny, and that I should stop being so selfish and realize that I was hurting Nancy. That's when we really started fighting. I told him he had taken away my best friend and broken my heart. He said he didn't care because he really liked Nancy and that I was being dumb! Nancy could be my friend and his, both. And why was I always sitting around like I had a pole sticking down the back of my dress? I told him that was how ladies sat. (What this had to do with Nancy and Betty, I really don't know.) And he told me I should stop trying to be what I'm not, and just be myself. That's when Mother opened the back door and ordered us inside. She was really mad! She said the entire neighbourhood could hear us arguing! And then she saw her good glassware and linen outside. I told her we couldn't expect guests to drink out of our everyday, ordinary chipped tumblers. She stood over me the entire time I washed the glasses to make sure "you do it right!" Then she made me soak the linens in salt and water to remove the raspberry stains. Honestly!

I wonder what Brian meant when he said I should just be myself. Who else could I be? I'm glad he went back to the farm tonight so I don't have to look at him.

Still haven't written to George.

Monday, August 13, 1945

Grandma won the "Little Dutch Girl" quilt and gave it to me! I couldn't believe it when she came over and handed it to me! She said she saw me admiring it at the picnic and thought I would like to have it. It's folded on the end of my bed right now and looks so swell.

Irma was at the hospital today and said that she thinks I'm right, that John is trying to drive her away. I told her maybe she should just ask him outright if he wants her to go, but she says she can't as she is afraid he'll say yes. Irma is so beautiful and sweet—I don't know how any man could let her go. I feel just like I'm Dorothy Dix giving advice.

Aunt Lily was over today and said she is going to start a secretarial course in September, and when she's finished, she'll work in an office. I greatly admire her for her ambitions. I hope Alex was listening. If I wasn't going to be a nurse, I'd be a secretary. I asked Aunt Lily if she and Sam had made up. She's been very quiet about him since Caroline's tea party. She said she and Sam are just friends, but they have gone out a few times recently and had a good time.

After she left, Mother told me I shouldn't have asked Aunt Lily about Sam, that it's none of my business. But then Mother went on to tell Dad that at the rate she was going, Aunt Lily would never get married and have children. (Which I think is also Aunt Lily's business!) Dad just grunted behind his newspaper, which made Mother mad. She said that Dad never listens to her and that maybe Lily's right and working rather than being married to a stick-in-the-mud is the way to go. Dad just grunted again, then laughed when Mother whipped off her apron and threw it at him. He grabbed her around the waist and pulled her down into his lap for a kiss. Honestly, my parents are so undignified. I can't imagine Betty's father kissing Betty's mother like that—and right in front of us kids!

After I worked, Betty, Lydia, and I went to the C.P.R. train station and cheered for a trainload of wounded that came in. There were five thousand people there to greet them! I nearly melted from the heat and crowds.

JAPAN QUITS WORLD AGAIN AT PEACE
—London Free Press, *August 14, 1945*

Tuesday, August 14, 1945

Japan surrendered! It's over! The entire war is over! I must get downtown right away!

Wednesday, August 15, 1945

Morning

There is to be a big street dance downtown tonight in front of the Armories on Dundas Street. It's a good thing the heat wave broke overnight or we'd all be sweltering crowded together! It's cool and sunny today.

I'm going to the dance with Rick. He and I and some of his friends went downtown yesterday and there were thousands of people filling the streets, just like at the VE celebrations in May. Lots of "blushing paper" was being thrown around. I cheered and yelled and screamed and am still quite hoarse this morning. I did feel sad that I wasn't with Nancy, like I was when we celebrated the end of the war in Europe. It got me thinking that I should end our own personal war, but I don't know how to surrender! Mother is correct. I do have a lot of pride. I wish it would "goeth," as she's always saying. But then I'd fall.

Today is my volunteer day at the hospital. I bet the men are excited.

Biggest crowd in London history throngs streets in VJ celebration.

—London Free Press, *August 15, 1945*

Wednesday, August 15, 1945

Late at night

Here is what happened at the street party:

I went downtown with Rick again. Brian said he was going with Nancy. (He got to come home from the farm for the day for the celebrations.) That made me feel sad, because last time Nancy and I went together.

Everyone in our family went downtown—except Alex, who went in to work, and Dad, who wasn't feeling too well. Dad said he'd take care of Baby Billy so Caroline could go to the celebration. He's quite sure the aircraft factory will close now that the war is over. Mother says he's worrying himself into an early grave. Aunt Lily, Mother, Caroline, and Irma went together.

We arrived down at the Armories to find Dundas Street completely packed with people from Wellington to Waterloo! I soon lost sight of Mother and the others, but I did see Stephen. Or rather I heard him! He was there with Brent and the Goddards, banging dishpans with wooden spoons. A military band was playing songs, but everyone was so crushed together we couldn't dance, so we sang instead. It was swell hearing everyone singing "Roll Out the Barrel."

Some of the men were drunk, and I got quite a shock when I saw Rick and his friends passing a bottle around. Rick asked me if I wanted a drink and I said no. Two of the other girls said yes. The party part was great fun. We wandered all over downtown and there were lots of bonfires lit and firecrackers going off. Rick and his friends got another bottle of some sort of drink from a soldier. I thought they were funny at first, but then it scared me as it got later and later and I knew Mother would be worried. I asked Rick to take me home and he said,

"Sure, Baby-face. I'd love to take you to my home," and everyone laughed except me.

Finally, I said I was going, and Rick said not to worry, he'd walk me home, he was just fooling around. Halfway home, Rick suddenly pulled me into some trees and started to kiss me. His lips were slipperier than usual, and it felt like he was swallowing the bottom half of my face. Then he actually grabbed my chest! I pushed his hand away, and he said, "Aw, come on, Baby-face, just a little cuddle. We've been going out all summer. All the other girls let their boyfriends touch them."

I didn't know what to do. I didn't want him to think I was a prude and I didn't want to lose him as a boyfriend, but I didn't want him touching me, either. Finally, I said Mother would be worried and I had to get home. At the end of our street, I told him I'd go home alone from there. Mother would have had a fit if she'd seen Rick had been drinking. I'm so confused.

Thursday, August 16, 1945

Brian went right back to the farm this morning. It is very important that the harvest get in, as our crops have to go to Europe to feed people who don't have homes or didn't get a crop planted themselves because of the war.

The evening newspaper says that the end of the war isn't going to mean that all the factories close. Mother left the newspaper open on the kitchen table so Dad would see it and stop worrying.

The newspaper also said that there would be more coke for furnaces to keep homes warm this winter, which also cheered Dad up. And he needs a lot of cheering up because there are still lots of rumours that the plant is going to close down, even though the managers keep denying it. Dad came home all worked up tonight, yelling that bosses were all just a bunch of criminals, making a profit on the backs of others and then discarding them when they didn't need them any more. Mother kept telling him to settle down and have his supper. He sat, but he didn't eat much. Just said, how on earth was he supposed to put food on the table for everyone if he didn't have a job? Stephen looked very scared.

I told Alex that this would be an excellent time for him to pursue some of those doorways of opportunity that the government was offering veterans now that the war had ended. He rolled his eyes.

I wish there was someone to talk to about Rick. And Alex. And Dad.

Friday, August 17, 1945

Boring day. Just worked in my garden. I wonder if the forget-me-nots will come back next year.

[Returning Japanese POWs] . . . *have told of a tremendous death rate from hardships, malnutrition, and lack of medical care for men who became so weak they could barely drag themselves along.*

—London Free Press, *August 20, 1945*

Saturday, August 18, 1945

I had to wheel a soldier who was a Japanese POW. He's one of the first ones we've seen. He was skinny as a rail even though he'd already been in care at a hospital out west. Someone said he had beriberi, a tropical disease, and probably parasites. I think he was pretty young, except he didn't look it. Most of his teeth were gone, which made his face look caved in and old. He trembled the entire time I wheeled him. I had to go into a linen closet and cry after I got him to his ward. We heard that the POWs had to build a railroad from Bangkok to Burma in terrible conditions. When I see someone like him, so badly treated by the Japanese army, I find it easy to hate the Japanese and not feel one bit sorry that they got a bomb dropped on them. But then I remember that the bomb killed lots of children, who didn't treat anyone badly.

One of the nursing sisters came in to get towels and saw me crying and gave me a hug. She said, "It's very sad, I know. But we have to keep heart. New treatments come out every day. We have penicillin now to help make bodies better, and maybe someday we'll have something to heal the mind, but for now remember, kindness and understanding go a long way, and you're an important part of that."

She made me feel better, but still my eyes kept dripping off and on all afternoon. I feel like all the sadness of the world is inside me today.

Sunday, August 19, 1945

I'm in the living room listening to a radio show with Dad this afternoon (and at the same time writing in my diary). It's pouring rain outside and there's not much else to do. Actually, I'm really waiting to see if Rick telephones me today. It's funny, but I'm not sure if I care whether he does or not.

Anyway, we're listening (I'm half listening) to a program *The Harbour Called Mulberry*. It's all about a great floating port that thirty thousand men made in a bunch of different factories in England, and on D-Day, all the parts were gathered together and towed to France and assembled at Normandy so the soldiers could land. It helped win the war. Imagine someone thinking to do that. I wish I was that smart.

It's nice just being here with Dad. He keeps saying, "Isn't that something, Bobby?" And I say, "Yes," though I don't know what he's talking about most of the time. It's just nice to be sitting with him.

Evening

I'm hiding in my bedroom because if looks could kill, I'd be dead right now. Aunt Lily, Grandma, and Irma came for supper, and I'd just bitten into a lovely cob of corn when Irma said John had been very rude to her at the hospital today and she had had it, so she was taking the bull by the horns and was going to do "what you said, Bobby."

That's when Mother shot me the look that could kill. "Now don't be too hasty, Irma," she said.

Rick never called.

Later

Mother came in a few minutes ago. She asked me what exactly I had said to Irma. I thought really hard but couldn't remember telling Irma anything. Then Mother said, "Irma said it was something about maybe John trying to make her hate him so she'll leave him."

Then I remembered what I had told Irma on the bus last week. "I was just thinking that out loud," I told Mother. "I didn't mean anything by it. It's just that he that acts like he doesn't want her around at all so I told her to ask him outright if he wanted her to leave so she'd know once and for all."

"You cannot meddle in other people's lives, Bobby," Mother said. "Particularly in their marriages. You could do a lot of harm."

Now I feel really bad. I hope I haven't ruined Irma's life.

Still no call from Rick. Now I do care.

*The large modern factory operated by Central Aircraft Ltd.
is to continue production of mosquito fuselages . . .*
—London Free Press, *August 20, 1945*

Monday, August 20, 1945

Mother had the newspaper folded right by Dad's breakfast this morning because there was an article about the factory definitely staying open. "Maybe that will make him feel better," she said.

Brian came home for supper as he was able to catch a ride from the farm. He looks very tanned and fit so I guess the flyers that said working on the harvest makes you healthy are right. He was smoking! Mother was not very pleased. He went to see Nancy this evening. Maybe Nancy will hate his smoking too, and they'll break up.

The man who was a Japanese POW was in the sunroom today. An older woman was visiting him. His mother, I expect. She kept dabbing at her eyes. He pretty much just smoked and stared out the window. It reminded me a lot of Alex when he first came home from the war and I visited him at the hospital. He wouldn't talk to me either. A lot of the men in here have shrapnel wounds or other hurts, but they are also hurt inside where you can't see, like Alex was—and still is. I know that now. I wonder how long it takes to make the brain better. Or *can* you make the brain better? It would be difficult to know because you can see a wound heal, but you can't see inside the brain.

And speaking of Alex, Brent came over to talk to him this evening. They sat in the backyard and smoked like before. Julia said it was good for Brent and Alex to be together. I asked her why and she said, "They've both been through the same thing. They understand how that feels."

I pointed out to her that Alex was in the army, and Brent was in the air force and a prisoner of war—what on earth did they have in common?

And Julia said, "Guilt, maybe. Guilt that they came back and others didn't. We weren't there so we can't understand that."

"Maybe they should just try to forget the war," I said.

"They'll never do that," Julia told me. "They'll live with it always."

I've been thinking about what Julia said. I thought soldiers and other people at the war would come back feeling very brave and *triumphant*, and be happy to be home, but I never thought they would come back feeling guilty. I feel guilty when I've done something wrong, but *they* didn't do anything wrong. It's so confusing. What's also confusing is that Julia seems to be getting smarter.

Tuesday, August 21, 1945

Today is Princess Margaret Rose's fifteenth birthday. I bet she got lots of presents. Princesses do.

Stephen got bitten on the hand by the Goddards' dog. I told Mother that Stephen could get rabies. She said the Goddards' dog was not rabid and its teeth barely broke the skin. I told her we'd soon find out when Stephen began foaming at the mouth. Mother very firmly pushed me out of the bathroom where she was bandaging Stephen's hand.

Rick just called! We're going out Thursday night. I still have a boyfriend.

> *Dr. J. R. Oppenheimer, one of the men chiefly responsible for the atomic bomb, was "a little scared of what we had made."*
>
> —London Free Press, *August 17, 1945*

> *The War Department has denied that radio-activity would*
> *persist after an atomic bomb explosion.*
>
> —London Free Press, *August 17, 1945*

Wednesday, August 22, 1945

The newspaper this morning said that people are continuing to die in Japan from radio-activity left over from the Atom bomb. I'm not sure what radio-activity is, though the newspaper says a lot of people have burns and blisters. The newspaper also said 30,000 to 60,000 people have now died from the Atom bomb (and more are dying every day) and 160,000 are injured. I can't begin to imagine that many people dead. I've only seen one dead person, Grandma Harrison, and she was in a casket. I can't imagine 60,000 people in caskets. Where would they bury them all? And how can the hospitals take care of all those who are hurt?

You think from the newspaper that war is all about the good people against the bad people, but there's a lot of in-between people who are neither good or bad. It's the in-between people who sometimes get hurt the most.

All I hope is that no one drops one of those bombs on us here in London, Ontario.

Evening

A wonderful day! I was volunteering at the hospital when Irma came and found me. She said she'd finally got the courage up to ask John outright if he was trying to get rid of her. She said at first he denied it, but then he said maybe he was. He said he didn't want her sticking with him now that he was scarred and ill just because she felt sorry for him, and that it wasn't fair she didn't get the man back she had married in the first place. She said she told him not to be silly because she loved him and she wanted to be with him "for better or for worse," as she'd promised when they got married. She said John was quiet for a while, then suddenly reached out and took her hand and kissed it. Irma said she knows that there are going to be hard days ahead and everything isn't going to be magically better, but "at least it's a start." She seemed so happy.

Hearing her tell it was like listening to a Hollywood movie.

Thursday, August 23, 1945

Caroline received her travel plans today. The Australian government said that it will be safe for the war brides to travel in the Pacific in September now that the war is over. She is to go to Toronto to the War Bride Centre in two weeks. From there she will go by train to Vancouver and then to San Francisco. She and 173 other war brides will leave September 27 on the SS *Matsonia* for Brisbane, Australia. James should be back in Australia by then.

Suddenly it seems very real that Caroline is leaving. I miss her already and she's not even left yet! Australia is very far away. I might not ever see her or Billy again. I asked Caroline who I was going to talk to when I needed to know about woman stuff. She said I should speak to Mother or Aunt Lily, or I could send a letter to her in Australia. The difficulty with that plan is that it takes forever to get letters and I might need an answer immediately. Why did she have to go and marry an Australian?

Friday, August 24, 1945

Very late

This page will probably have smears all over it because I can't stop crying. I broke up with Rick tonight.

Here is what happened:

Rick didn't have enough money for the show, so we got ice cream cones and went for a walk. It was a lovely night, warm, stars glimmering up above, and I felt so happy to have a boyfriend to hold my hand. After we were done our cones, Rick took me to the children's playground. It was getting dark now, but he pushed me on the swings and I thought I'd burst with joy because it was so romantic.

Then he pulled me down to sit beside him on a bench. That's when he started to nuzzle my neck, and kiss me, and his hand went straightaway to my chest. I managed to get my lips off his and I slapped his hand away from my front and said, "Did you hear about how many Japanese people are dying from radio-activity from the Atom bomb?"

"What do you care?" he said. "They're just Japs."

And that's when I realized that I really didn't like Rick at all. He may be good looking, but he's not very smart and he's not very nice. He's just one of those boys Dorothy Dix is always warning girls about—boys with only one thing on their mind. I asked him to take me home and he said, "What the HELL is the matter with you?" He actually swore at me. I felt like I had been slapped.

I said I didn't want to see him any more. I told him I wasn't the kind of girl he obviously thought I was, as he kept wanting to touch my chest. He said I thought I was too smart for him with all my talk about radio-activity and I must be a Jap lover if I was so worried about them dying. And he *stalked* off, leaving me by myself in the park. I cried all the way home in the dark— by myself.

I tried to sneak in the kitchen door and into my bedroom, but Alex and Julia were in the kitchen having tea and saw me. Alex said, "I thought you were out with that kid, Rick."

I told him we'd broken up and burst into tears again.

"Did he take advantage of you?" Alex demanded.

That was the most upset I've ever seen him. And I didn't even think he cared about me very much any more.

Dad heard the commotion and turned off the radio and he

nearly blew a gasket that Rick had let me walk home alone at night. And then Alex and Dad thought they'd go find Rick and set him straight, so I yelled for Mother. She came flying in, buttoning her housecoat, and asked me if I was all right. I told her I was, but she had to stop Alex and Dad going for Rick. I'd never live that down if anyone found out my dad and brother had gone to beat up my old boyfriend.

Mother said for everyone to calm down and she'd take care of everything. She pushed Dad into his chair and made him promise not to move out of it while she and I talked. Then we went into my room. I was a bit scared, and so embarrassed telling her that Rick wanted to kiss all the time and I didn't. It felt like I had done something wrong, though I knew I hadn't. Then I asked her if that made me a prude. Mother said absolutely not. It made me a responsible young woman. She said I had acted quite properly and she was very proud of me. That made me feel a bit better. And she said that there were always boys like Rick out there, and now that I knew that first-hand, I could watch out for them. She said there were lots of really nice boys, too.

Then Julia filled the bathtub up for me and now I'm warm and in bed, but I still feel quite sad and teary (which is why this page is a bit smudged). Dad is still thundering around the house saying he's going to talk to "that boy's father." Mother just brought me a cup of tea.

Saturday, August 25, 1945

Another awful day. I have no friends at all! Here is what happened:

After work today, Betty, Lydia, and I went to the movies, but I was still so upset by Rick that I can't even remember what the picture was about. Even though Mother said I wasn't, I worried the entire time that I really was a prude, like Rick said.

When we got back to Betty's and were sitting in her back-yard with glasses of lemonade, I asked Betty and Lydia what they would do if a boy touched them in a place they weren't supposed to be touched. That's when Betty squealed, "Oh, Bobby, has Rick touched you THERE?" I told them I wasn't asking for me, it was a *hypothetical* question.

And Betty said, "So he did touch you! You better be careful. You don't want to end up like your sister, Caroline." She whispered that last bit, though I don't know why. Her backyard is so big no one could overhear us.

"What's wrong with Caroline?" I demanded.

"Lydia. What's wrong with Caroline?" I asked, because Betty didn't seem to want to answer.

Lydia shrugged, slurped her drink, and avoided looking at either of us, not wanting to take sides. She has absolutely no backbone!

"Well, you know," Betty said, "Caroline had to get married and all."

"She and James love each other," I said. "And it worked out all right. She's going to Australia, you know! It's not like he's leaving her here on her own."

"Well, no man likes to be pushed into marriage. Maybe she shouldn't go to Australia. In fact, what if he deserts her there?" Betty said.

"His parents already wrote Caroline, and they have a house built for them and everything. He even told Mother and Dad how much he loves Caroline and he sent her flowers for Mother's Day." Now I'm crying again, thinking of the awful things Betty said. I feel like I've cried for a month!

I left right after I told Betty I never wanted to speak to her or Lydia again. Brian is right. Betty has only empty air upstairs. Now I have no girl OR boy friends. I am doomed to a lonely, loveless life. It is a good thing I have my nursing career to focus on. I wish I could write George. He'd never say, "They're just Japs." He'd care—about them, and me, and Alex and Brent and Nancy. But I don't know what to say after not writing him so long. I really need Nancy to be my friend. I'm going to cry again.

Sunday, August 26, 1945

Brian and Alex disappeared right after lunch today. Mother asked me if I knew where they'd gone, but I told her I had no idea. "They had their heads together for a bit first," Mother said. And she frowned. Mother has a sixth sense that tells her when her kids are in trouble or up to no good.

Mother is having a special supper tonight so Brian can say goodbye to Caroline as he has to go back to the farm first thing tomorrow morning. Mother reminded Brian that school starts September 10. Stephen goes back September 4, but high school starts later because the farmers need the students' help for harvesting. Before he disappeared, Brian told me he was sorry that Rick had treated me so badly and wanted me to know that not all guys act like that.

Brent came over to see Alex this afternoon, but Alex wasn't back yet from wherever he went with Brian. Brent stayed for a few minutes to speak to Dad. Brent smoked constantly and looked quite thin, with dark circles under his eyes. When he left, I went with him out to the sidewalk. Brent told me to say hello to Alex for him, and to tell Alex to take care. He also told me to patch things up with Nancy as soon as I can. He said that Nancy has her fair share of pride also, and both of us will have to meet halfway if we are to be friends again.

Then he said the oddest thing. He said, "War takes an ordinary man and puts a gun in his hand and asks him to do something extraordinary—to kill. And the first time that person points the gun at another human being and fires, he is changed. Changed forever. Never forget that, Bobby." I think he was talking about Alex.

Monday, August 27, 1945

My reputation is in tatters! At the hospital today, one of the volunteers who goes to my school, though I don't know her too well, snickered when I walked by, not once, but twice. So I asked one of the student nurses what the big joke was.

The student nurse was embarrassed and didn't want to say anything at first, but then she said she'd heard some talk among the volunteers about me and a boy, but she didn't know anything further.

I was mortified. I held my head high all day to show I didn't care what anyone said, though now my neck is stiff and sore.

Even though I said I'd never speak to Lydia again, I stopped off at her house on my way home, because I couldn't think of anyone else to ask what was going on. And after all it was Betty who said horrible things about Caroline, not Lydia. She led me to the front porch so no one would overhear us talking. She said that Rick was telling everyone that I'd let him go "all the way" with me, and that I was always bugging him to go out, even though he said he didn't want to have anything to do with me any more. I felt like I'd been slapped in the face.

I told her I broke up with HIM and I certainly never let him have "his way" with me. Lydia said she believed me, though I'm not sure if she really did. Lydia is wishy-washy, going along with what anyone says. She has absolutely no backbone.

I also know now where Alex and Brian went Sunday. They went to see Rick. Alex said they just talked to him, though he had to stop Brian from popping Rick one on the nose! Then

Dad said that after church he'd talked to "that young man's father and set him straight about leaving a girl to walk home alone in the dark," and that Rick's father was very upset with Rick. That's when I got really angry and yelled at Dad and Alex (and I would have yelled at Brian if he'd been here) that they had all ruined my life! That Rick was lying about me because they'd meddled in my business and made him mad. And worse, everyone was believing him. Then Mother said not to worry because my real friends would not believe Rick. I told her I didn't have any real friends any more. I also told her I was never going to go back to the hospital or school!

Monday, August 27, 1945

Evening

Brent has left London without telling anyone, other than leaving a note. In the note he said he was fine, but he was going out west to see more of the country and to decide what to do with his life. Mother said Mrs. Rev. Goddard and Nancy are very upset, but Rev. Goddard didn't seem surprised, as he'd felt Brent might leave. I don't think I am surprised either, remembering what Brent said to me on Sunday. Nancy must feel just awful. I vow I will go tomorrow and humbly ask her to be my friend again. We've been apart too long. Except, what if she heard the rumours about Rick and me? Maybe she won't want to be my friend.

I've been thinking a lot about what Brent said before he left. I see now that Alex has changed forever and there is nothing I can do about it, no matter how much I want to. It's up to Alex. I also think Julia understands that and that is why she doesn't push him to be ambitious. Maybe she is just right for Alex after all, though I hate to admit it. Just realizing that makes me feel lighter, like someone lifted a weight off my shoulders.

It's very, very cold tonight! It's only forty degrees out. I'll need my blanket!

Ottawa closes Central Aircraft. Only a few of 875 London workers will keep jobs.
—London Free Press, *August 28, 1945*

Tuesday, August 28, 1945

I can't stop crying. Dad is in the hospital. I think he is going to die. Here is what happened:

Mother, Grandma, and I were canning tomatoes when Dad arrived home in the middle of the morning with terrible news. Central Aircraft has shut down. He got seven days' pay and was told to apply for unemployment income. He was dreadfully upset. He kept saying he didn't know how he was going to put food on the table, and Mother kept assuring him we'd just tighten our belts. "We've been in tough spots before and have come through just fine. We will again," Mother said.

It didn't help at all that Grandma put in her two cents' worth and said, "You'll lose the house. I expect you'll all be at my door looking for a place to stay."

That's when I told Grandma she had a spot on her neck and I thought it might be the beginning of shingles or scabies and she should go home and rest. (It was the only time Mother didn't threaten to take away my medical book.)

After Grandma left, Dad went out to the garage. Mother went to Aunt Lily's to get more salt for canning and told me to make some sandwiches. After the sandwiches were made, I sent Stephen to the garage to get Dad for lunch. Stephen came running back in, screaming that Dad was sick. I raced out to the garage and Dad was lying on the cement floor, clutching his chest! He'd had a spell of some kind.

I ran into the house and telephoned Aunt Lily to bring her car over. Then I grabbed a blanket from the sofa and ran back out to the garage and covered Dad. I remembered that the home medical book said you should always keep patients warm. Dad could barely speak, but he gasped out that his chest hurt. That's when Mother and Aunt Lily arrived. I told Mother I thought Dad was having a heart attack. She said it was probably severe indigestion from him being so upset, but I told her he needed to go to the hospital right away. Somehow we got Dad into the car.

It's been three hours since they left and Stephen and I are curled up on the sofa next to the telephone waiting for it to ring. I made him some cocoa because even though it is a warm day, his teeth were chattering. I feel cold too, but writing here helps to keep my mind busy. Irma is watching Baby Billy so Caroline can be at the hospital with Mother.

I telephoned the farm where Brian is staying and the farmer's wife said she'd let him know right away. I have no idea where Alex is, but I just realized that if Dad is out of work, Alex is too. I hope he's all right.

Tuesday, quite late, or very early Wednesday morning

Dad *did* have a heart attack. Mother says the doctors won't know how bad it is for a couple of days. I don't want Dad to die. I can't believe I yelled at him so much yesterday. I know he spoke to Rick's father because he was worried about ME. But I upset him. I probably caused his heart attack.

I'm on the couch in the living room because I have to share my bed with Grandma. She insists on sleeping at our house tonight to keep an eye on us while Mother is at the hospital. Aunt Lily and Alex are at the hospital too, keeping Mother company. I told Grandma we'd be perfectly fine on our own, but she said she should stay. She whistles through her nose while she sleeps, then snorts, and it keeps me awake.

Brian got home about suppertime. He's on the front porch right now, pacing back and forth. I think he's smoked about a hundred cigarettes.

Stephen just came out of his room. He wants to sleep with me on the couch. He used to sleep with me when the war was on and he was scared. We're both scared now, so I told him he could sleep here. Please God, don't let Dad die. If You keep him alive I'll never be mean to anyone again in my life. I won't ever backtalk Mother or yell, or gossip or fight with Brian, and I'll help all the time. I won't be proud or vain. I'll even clean the garage for Dad. Just don't let him die.

Thursday, August 30, 1945

Morning

Yesterday passed in a blur. Caroline, Aunt Lily, Alex, and Grandma have all been up to the hospital, but I'm not allowed to go as I'm too young. I think that is very unfair, even though Caroline told me she, Grandma, and Aunt Lily didn't see Dad at all but sat in the waiting room. Alex was allowed in with Mother because he's the oldest son.

At least Grandma has gone back to her own bed—thank goodness. Julia told Grandma that the stress of taking care of us might make Grandma ill and add to Mother's worry, so Grandma went home. That was very smart of Julia.

Julia's been a big help. She took time off work to be with us. She's very calm and sensible, while we're all running around like chickens with our heads cut off. She's taking care of all of us, even me. I tried to pretend at first that I was fine and didn't need any taking care of, because nurses shouldn't get upset, but my eyes kept dripping while I washed dishes or made lunch. Finally, Julia sat me down with a cup of tea. I told her all about how grey and drawn Dad looked lying on the garage floor, and she told me that I'd had a terrible shock and couldn't expect to feel well for a bit. She made me go and lie down, but I can't settle, so I'm writing in here to keep my brain busy.

Irma has been a wonderful help too, taking care of Baby Billy. She even took him up to the hospital to visit John. She said John took to Baby Billy immediately and they had a lovely visit, and I could see the hope in her eyes that she might have a Baby Billy of her own someday.

I miss George. I miss his lopsided smile, his kind eyes, his gentle voice—everything about him. I wish he was here because he'd understand about my yelling at Dad. I think I'll write to him right now and ask him to forgive me. I really miss him. My eyes are dripping again. Swell. Now there are splotches of ink all over the page.

Thursday, August 30, 1945

Nancy and I are friends again. Here is how it happened:

Just before lunch, the doorbell rang and I went to answer it, and Nancy was standing there. I told her that Brian was at the hospital and I'd let him know she'd called. She said she hadn't come to see Brian, but to see me. I started to cry AGAIN—it seems that is all I've done for the past three days! I sobbed as I told Nancy I had wanted to be her friend for half the summer, but I didn't know how to apologize for how awful I was to her. She said, "You just did, Bobby." And then she apologized for not realizing how I would feel when she went out with Brian and that she should have told me first. We sat all afternoon and talked. Or at least, I talked.

I told her I was sorry Brent went away.

Nancy said she was feeling better now about Brent going. "He never did like being held down in one place," Nancy said. "It's probably better for him to go away for a while to figure out what he wants to do."

And I told her I had planned to come over a couple days ago

and ask her to be my friend again, but I was afraid that she wouldn't want to because of my reputation. She said she'd rather be friends with someone who had a reputation, because that was much more interesting than being friends with a milksop like Betty or Lydia.

Then we discussed the entire Rick problem, and that I hadn't done ANYTHING, but I couldn't face going to school or back to the hospital. Nancy said we should tar and feather Rick and run him out of town for telling lies. She said of course I hadn't done anything, and to remember that gossip is only a seven-day wonder and everyone will have forgotten about it by next week and I shouldn't let other people's wagging tongues keep me from what I liked doing.

Then I told her how I'd stopped writing George for the summer, but finally last night had written him a huge letter telling him everything, but I wasn't sure if I should mail it. It was sitting on my dresser all ready to go. Nancy said I should send it, because George would completely understand.

I told her how sloppy Rick kissed and how it felt like he was swallowing my face and we had a good giggle together. (I did not ask what Brian's kisses are like. In fact, I didn't ask her anything about Brian, and Nancy kept off the subject too. I'm just going to pretend they don't kiss at all.) I hugged her hard and told her I had missed her so much.

Thursday, August 31, 1945

I heard Mother crying in her bedroom last night. I looked all through my *A to Z Home Medical Book*, but I couldn't find anything to cure heartache.

Thursday, August 31, 1945

Evening

Dad is out of the woods! Mother came home from the hospital for supper and told us Dad will be fine. Then Mother cried and cried, and I started crying, then Stephen, then Caroline and Aunt Lily, and Julia, and I think even Alex and Brian had tears in their eyes. We're lucky we didn't flood the house! Thank you so much, God, for not letting Dad die. I will keep all my promises.

I can't find the letter I wrote to George. It doesn't matter as I'm too ashamed to send it anyway.

Friday, August 31, 1945

People have been dropping off casseroles and cookies and cakes for us most of the day. Mother says we'll never be able to eat it all, but it's lovely to know we have so many friends.

Dad will be in the hospital for three weeks, then he will need a few months of rest at home. I imagine Mother will tie him to a chair and not let him out of her sight after this. Mother will be very busy for the next few weeks, and she said that Alex is head of the household until Dad gets back, and we're to mind him, and Julia also.

Caroline told Mother she doesn't feel right going to Australia when Dad isn't well, and that she feels she contributed to Dad's heart attack. I wish I had known that Caroline feels that way because she should know *I* caused it, not her. Mother said Caroline has to go and start her life with James, and Dad understands that and wants Caroline to be happy.

Stephen asked Mother if we are going to be poor because Dad can't work. Mother told him not to worry, we will be fine, and that's when Brian told Mother he's not going back to school this year. It seems the farmer thinks quite highly of Brian and wants to keep him on as permanent help. What's stranger still is that it seems that Brian really likes the country! Mother nearly had a fit and told Brian it was out of the question, he has to go back to school.

Brian said, "I can help bring in some money for a bit. I'm not going back. I'm not the smart one around here. *She* is!" And he pointed right at me! I nearly fell off my chair in shock. "She's the one with the brains. She's the one who needs to go to school."

I didn't know anyone thought I had brains!

Mother said she doesn't want to worry Dad about Brian right now, so she gave him permission to take a year off school, and when the year is up, they will talk about his returning next year.

I found out where Alex went after the plant closed. In all the commotion we'd forgotten that he had disappeared! Alex went to see Julia's father, who is swamped with orders to build houses for all the returning veterans and their families. Alex said that construction will be booming, and Julia's father hired Alex to be a supervisor. Alex says it is a really good job. (Alex says Dad can probably work for the construction company too, when he gets better. Mother says knowing that will go a long way to easing Dad's worries about money!)

I must go. Julia and I are going to clean the ENTIRE house for Mother as a treat. It's the least I can do. Julia is not such a bad sort after all. I've not thought of her as a mouse for a long time.

Saturday, September 1, 1945

I went to work this afternoon, and everyone was really nice and told me they hope Dad gets better soon. No one even mentioned Rick. Nancy even switched her volunteer day from Sunday to today so she could be there with me.

Sunday, September 2, 1945

Only Mother and I went to church this morning. Stephen went to Sunday School. Brian is back at the farm. It felt strange with just the two of us, and Mother must have felt the same way because when we sat down in the pew she suddenly grabbed my hand and squeezed it.

Walking home from church, I told Mother I hated the way things were changing. I hated Caroline going away, Dad being ill, the aircraft plant closing, Brian leaving school, Alex being a construction supervisor. I told her I even hated the war being over in one way, because it caused so much change. Mother said that there was no magic to take us back to yesterday. Life changes constantly and we just have to accept that and continue to look forward to tomorrow.

That's when I told her how bad I felt that I'd caused Dad's heart attack. She stopped right on the street and grabbed my shoulders and gave me a little shake and said I was not to blame myself as Dad's heart had been bad for quite a while. She said his heart attack was no one's fault, and then she said that I probably saved Dad's life by recognizing that he was having a heart attack and getting Aunt Lily over right away and insisting he go to the hospital. She said I kept my head and that maybe my reading the medical book wasn't a bad idea after all.

I asked her, if it wasn't my fault, did I have to keep all the promises I made to God to keep Dad alive? She said it was probably a good idea to keep them anyway.

And then she said I was really outgrowing my clothes, including my underwear, and she'd take me downtown to get new ones before school starts. I told her I know exactly what size I am. I am not getting naked and trying on brassieres in that store ever again! I was never so embarrassed in my life as I was last year when Mother made me fit them on right in the store!

Monday, September 3, 1945

School for Stephen tomorrow. I start next week. Dad has agreed that Brian can have a year off to work since he wants to try it.

I had a long talk with Alex today on the front porch. The most we've talked since he got home from overseas. I asked him if he was sure he wanted to be supervisor of a construction company, and didn't he want to be a newspaper writer like he wanted before the war? He stared at me a long time, then excused himself and went into the house. I thought he was mad at me, but he came right back with something in his hand. He held out the diary I gave him last year at the hospital. It hadn't been used.

"I'm not the writer, Bobby, you are. You're always scribbling ideas and feelings in your old notebook and collecting interesting words. You're not a nurse, Bobby. You're a writer! You need this book more than I do."

I took the diary from him and asked him if he was sure.

"I'm happy to be working on houses for families," Alex said. "It's nice to do something that's productive and useful. It helps to make up for the fact I disgraced myself when I came home with battle fatigue."

I started to protest, but Alex waved it off. "Sure, I had a leg wound, but it's shameful coming home because I didn't have the courage to do what had to be done, and instead went off my head. But to be building something new, and not destroying, is going to help me feel better. Bobby, I know you have an idea of what I am in your head, but it's no longer real. This is who I am."

"What's in my head is that you're a hero," I told him. "It's not important how you came back from the war, it's that you went over there in the first place. You volunteered to go because you thought it was the right thing to do. That's what's in my head. You've always been my hero, Alex, and that's never going to change."

Alex gave me a huge hug, the first real hug he's given me since he got home from overseas.

Thursday, September 6, 1945

Caroline and Baby Billy left today for their trip to Australia. Stephen and I ran all the way down the railway platform waving at her until the train was just a speck in the distance. She promised to send me postcards all the way across Canada on the train. I miss her so much already.

Dad comes home in nine days.

Saturday, September 15, 1945

I have the whole house to myself this afternoon. Mother is at the hospital picking up Dad to come home and Stephen is at the Goddard's and Brian is back at the farm, so I'm sitting on the front porch writing in my new diary.

I started school last Monday. Nancy held my arm all the way. Earlier, we had discussed at great length whether I should ignore Rick entirely, or speak to him icily, or pretend nothing happened. We finally decided I would be pleasant, but cool. We thought that might confuse him the most. And stop people talking. Our plan worked swimmingly. I must admit, though, that a small part of me is pleased as punch that I can be looked upon as a worldly woman of experience. Neither Betty nor Lydia can say that!

My new diary is lovely. The pages are smoother than the ones in my Math notebook and it makes me feel like a real writer to have a book to write in. When I told Mother that Alex gave me back the diary, and that I wanted to be a writer and not a nurse, she gave me one of Dad's fountain pens. She told me Dad would want me to have it, but she made me give her back the *A to Z Home Medical Book* as a trade. I really didn't mind. I don't think I was cut out to be a nurse anyway, though I really like the sweet little caps the nurses get to wear.

One part of me is sad that I'm not going to be a nurse because I thought I could really help people. But I think I can help people as a writer. I could be like the "gal correspondents," like May Craig, or Margaret Bourke-White, who wrote about the war, and I could travel all over the world as a reporter and tell people what REALLY happens. Maybe people would read what I write and never forget how horrible war really is, and that would stop them from ever having another one. That would be almost as helpful as being a nurse. I guess I've changed, too, like everything else, but I think I'm going to like this change—being a writer!

Must go, someone is coming up the sidewalk.

Saturday, September 15, 1945

Late at night

GOSH! GOSH! AND TRIPLE GOSH! Today was the best day of my entire life—so far! Here is what happened:

I stopped writing because someone was coming up the walk. Then I heard my name called. It was GEORGE! GEORGE!

I was so surprised, I couldn't say a single word, I just sat there with my mouth gaping. He looked so nice in a brown suit, with his lopsided grin and kind grey eyes.

"Have you forgotten me?" he asked.

He said he knew it wasn't my sixteenth birthday yet, but as soon as he got my letter, he climbed on the next train and came to see me because he knew I was going through a very difficult time. That's when I started to cry. I cried all over him and couldn't stop. I must have some kind of eye disease (but as Mother took back her *A to Z Home Medical Book*, I can't look it up) because I cry when I'm sad and I cry when I'm happy. I leak tears constantly. I still can't believe he's here!

We had a good visit together before the others got home. I had no idea how my letter got sent to him, but I didn't tell him that. He told me all about his accounting course and what it's like to go to college and his plans for the future. I told him about the Nazi boy tied to the stake, and how it bothered me that so many Japanese people had been killed, and he listened and didn't even seem to mind that I was talking so much. George held my hand almost the entire afternoon and I didn't even need to put my Etiquette deodorant on it, because my palm didn't get sweaty even once.

Mother invited Irma, Aunt Lily, Grandma, and Nancy for supper. We had a wonderful time celebrating Dad's return home and George's surprise visit. Mother handed everyone a plate, and I noticed she'd cut George's meat for him so he wouldn't feel awkward. I really love Mother.

It turned out that Nancy had seen the letter to George on my dresser and thought she would mail it for me as I was so upset about Dad. I wondered where that letter had gone!

After supper George said he had to go and get a room at the YMCA, but Aunt Lily insisted that he stay at her place, in Caroline's old room. Grandma didn't think that was too proper, but Aunt Lily pooh-poohed her and that is where George is staying, for one lovely week. Mother even said I could take two days off school as George came such a long way to see me! I really, *really* love Mother.

After supper, George and I walked Nancy to her house. On our way home, I apologized for not writing him. I told him a little about Rick and what a confusing summer it had been.

George let go of my hand and for one horrible minute I thought he was mad at me, but he reached into his pocket and took out a small wrapped parcel and put it in my hand. I unwrapped it and there, mounted in a little frame, under glass, were the dried forget-me-nots that I had sent to him early in the summer. "I would be lying if I said I didn't think that maybe you had forgotten me," he said. "But I could never forget you, Bobby."

P.S. George's kisses are not sloppy!

> *Just think what this war is costing, too big to even imagine, but I believe the price is meagre when the countries prefer freedom than having the Nazis or Japan rule the land and the people being forced to give everything to them.*
>
> *—Lawrence Haworth, October 1944*

> *They fought on the beaches, in the cities and into the hills. They came from farms and from factories; from schools and from offices; from the ranks of the rich and the poor. Many did not return. Thousands carry the mark of sacrifice on their battered bodies. Still others will come home with memories of horror they will carry with them to their dying day. To all of them, Canada owes an unpayable debt.*
>
> *—Jack Park,* London Free Press, *May 8, 1945*

Bobby's Word List
In order of appearance

influence	hysteria
ambition	scandalous
glowered	dilemma
journalist	pungent
unique	endearments
trite	infuriated
abscess	halitosis
debut	suffused
bursitis	rambunctious
edible	fortitude
distraught	suffragette
ennui	virtue
heinous	enticing
skulking	triumphant
flabbergasted	stalked
epiphany	hypothetical
exhilarating	forlorn

Author's Note

The year 2005 marks the 60th anniversary of the end of World War II. As veterans age, fewer are left to share their memories and to tell us how it really was. World War II changed the world forever—from women entering the workforce to new medical discoveries to the way war is waged. But what doesn't change is the toll on people caught in war: the sacrifice of lives put on hold, sometimes for years; the emotional and physical wounds that never heal; and the sorrow when loved ones are sent away and do not come back. We must never forget.

Acknowledgements

Victory photos on page i are courtesy of Tune Family Fonds, the University of Western Ontario Archives, London, Ontario.

Newspaper quotations are courtesy of *The London Free Press*, London, Ontario.

Many thanks to Judy Ann Sadler for reading the manuscript and liking it. Thank you also to my editor, Lynne Missen, and my agent, Scott Treimel, for their support.